Sleeping to Death

Sleeping to Death

G.D. Baum

ISBN: 1494744325
ISBN 13: 9781494744328
Library of Congress Control Number: 2013923391
CreateSpace Independent Publishing Platform
North Charleston, South Carolina

To order additional copies, please contact.
BookSurge, LLC
www.booksurge.com
1-866-308-6235
orders@booksurge.com

Sleeping to Death

Dedicated to:

Henry Miller, for taking me down the road less travelled and

♉

Robert B. Parker, for pointing out the signpost called Mystery

CHAPTER ONE

Pauline and I were not exactly making love—more like wrestling with benefits.

This past year, she had increased the intensity of her weight training. Now, every time I made my way on top of her, she would shift her hips and roll me to the side, pinning my wrists over my head and somehow ending up on top again. Once securely in position, she would mash her lips against mine, blanketing us in blond hair.

We both knew it was a losing battle. Our main issue was that she had the temerity not to be my deceased wife, Janice. We had tried talking it out, which inevitably drifted into an immersion course on the many ways I was being unfair to her.

Of course, she was right. It was unfair of me to resent the fact that Pauline was here and Janice was not. It was not her fault. But in my defense, there was no one else to blame.

The phone rang. I tried to unravel myself. "Got to answer that," I said.

"What?"

"The phone."

She let go of my wrists. I rolled over, checking the Caller ID. It was my primary bodyguarding client, Susan Heung. "Yes, Susan?"

"Not Susan. It's Cho."

"I'm in the middle of something here, Cho."

"Susan's brother was just found dead at Rahway Prison."

I dislodged myself from Pauline and sat up, writing the time and the words *Brother—Jason Heung—Rahway* on a small legal pad. "How did he die?"

Pauline stabilized herself on all fours and slapped her hand on the pillow, mouthing the words, "Fuck it." She reared up on her knees and ran her hands through her hair a bunch of times, shaking it out.

"Burned up like garbage, literally," Cho said. "They recovered the body from the prison disposal bin."

"Susan must be in a state."

He paused. "My fiancée doesn't know I'm calling you yet. She's too busy doing what she always does, working the phones for information."

"Which is kind of useless, since you and I both know the obvious suspect for something like this."

"You think by some wild coincidence Cousin Bodacious might have had something to do with killing a Heung?"

"Just a random thought," I said, writing at the bottom of the pad, *Suspect—Cousin Bodacious / Newark*.

"There are implications. You gotta confirm it before she starts something she won't be able to stop."

"You want me to see Lt. Attia tomorrow morning?"

"Absolutely."

"How about I swing by your and Susan's townhouse in the meantime? She could be a target too."

"I can protect her," he said. "Just go see Attia first thing."

"Fine, but I don't think this is going anywhere. I assume Bodacious has already put in place all the boundaries between him and whoever did this. Even if we confirm it was him, there'll never be a prosecution."

"I agree."

I brought the receiver closer. "You tell Susan that?"

"No, and neither will you."

Pauline had put on her red, half-moon reading glasses and was leaning over to check the time. I stroked her bare bottom. She pulled away. "None of this makes any sense," I said. "What set Bodacious off now? Jason has been in prison for over a year."

"No idea. And one more thing. After you see Lt. Attia, maybe you can also go down with Susan to identify the body. I can't. My campaign is going to re-launch in three months."

"Of course."

"Thanks."

I hung up the phone. Pauline was standing by the bed, cinching her terry cloth robe. "Something happen to Susan's brother, the prick?" she said.

"Murdered."

"Good. She wants you to find out who did it, even though you already know who did it."

"I think I know."

She went to the bathroom, leaving the door slightly ajar. "But Cho and Susan's wedding is still going forward."

"We didn't get that far," I called out.

I heard her begin to pee. "Gyno said I need to start doing this immediately after to avoid urinary tract infections."

"You may proceed."

"Looking for his killer is going to be a fool's errand," she said.

"Then I'm just the man for the job."

CHAPTER TWO

On my way to see Lt. Attia that morning, I performed my daily check on Grandfather and his wife, April. I arrived at her small house on River Road in Edgewater just after 6:00 a.m. I knew she would be up. Her shift at the dungeon had ended only an hour before.

April met me at the door in work clothes: a black miniskirt with shiny, latex, thigh-high boots and a brushed iron necklace with the word "Kneel" hanging from its center. She was a wisp of a woman with brown eyes and matching thick, straight hair that reached below her hips.

"Just the man I want to see," she said, stepping aside to let me in. Their living room was strewn with toys and video games. She swayed side to side, holding her four-year-old son, Fletcher, in both arms. He had April's nose and fingers and Grandfather's Asian jet-black hair and eyes.

Fletcher was sleeping. His cheek rested against a white towel on her shoulder. His small hand clenched and unclenched the soft cloth.

"I'm on my way to the Police Department," I said. "Just wanted to quickly check in on Grandfather."

"He's been asleep now for about twenty hours, exactly like I left him yesterday afternoon."

"In other words, situation normal."

"When does that become a coma?" she said.

"Never. It's not a coma."

"Yeah, sure, this conversation again," she yawned over the words, covering her mouth with the back of her hand. Her nails were painted dark red with black tips. "Can you wake him? I'd like to say hello before I get some sleep."

"The needles still in the drawer?"

"I don't touch them."

He was in the upstairs bedroom laying on top of the green, goose down covers. His tangle of gray hair was spread out, as if submerged underwater.

Though we called him Grandfather, there were no grandchildren. The genesis of his name was buried in a dozen apocryphal stories. His wife, April, was thirty years younger. They had only married a few years ago.

His breathing was deep and flowing. It gently rocked his head on the pillow. I washed my hands twice and opened his cedar dragon box, taking out seven of the fine acupuncture needles.

April came to the doorway. She had replaced the towel on her shoulder with a different one. Fletcher made some sounds, and she increased the pace of her gentle rocking to quiet him. "What if he just doesn't wake up for say, a month?" she said.

"Think positive." I inserted acupuncture needles in Heart 7 and Spleen 6. They were general *chi* points that related to sleep. I waited a few moments and adjusted them by gently twisting between my index finger and thumb. I felt a faint energy wash over my hand, wrist, and finally, about half way up my arm. I placed five more needles along the meridian for lethargy.

I closed my eyes and meditated next to him. After about twenty minutes, I removed all the needles.

"What now?" April's voice startled me. I had forgotten she was there.

I placed them in an alcohol solution. "I'm headed to the Fort Lee Police Department to see Lt. Attia."

"Some conversation before you go?"

"I just wanted to stop by quickly, April."

"So that's a yes. Let me tuck the munchkin in first. I'll make tea."

⚬⚬⚬

She sat in her kitchen at the opposite end of their blond wood chopping block table. As she leaned in to take a sip, her hair fell forward, covering her face. It reminded me of Pauline. "Long night. Lots of kooks," she said.

"Any marks?"

"You want me to strip so you can inspect the merchandise?"

"Always."

She smiled. "Nothing exciting. Just some slight redness on my butt. No big deal."

"For a trained professional."

"As they say, don't try this at home."

"Because if they do, it might put you out of business."

She stroked her thigh. "So, why are you going to the police?" she said.

"Susan's brother, Jason, got himself murdered in prison. By the way, you knew him?"

"He came to the dungeon a bunch of times. Nasty and arrogant as I remember. Hated women. Who did it? I'd like to give him a medal."

"Popular thinking says Cousin Bodacious out of Newark for obvious reasons."

"Forget the medal. I stay away from that crowd."

"Smart."

"So, case closed?"

"Perhaps." I stirred my tea, swirling the small pieces of leaves to the top. I watched them settle in slow motion. "I didn't see anyone in front of the house when I came in," I said. "Is that a good sign?"

She leaned back in her chair. "I bet at least one of them is there by now. Tell me I'm wrong."

I walked to the window and parted the curtain. A Japanese man was kneeling on the front lawn, eyes closed, with a thin incense stick between his palms. He wore a brown and yellow Buddhist robe. His head was shaved. "You're wrong," I said.

"Bullshit," she said, closing her eyes. "Listen, before you go, would you please get rid of him?"

"You know, there's no really getting rid of any of them," I said, sitting again at the table.

She flicked her hair away from her forehead. "Help a girl out, okay? Just judo him off my lawn."

"If he leaves, there'll just be others who'll take his place."

"Lock, come on, just get him to move temporarily so I don't have to see him when I walk out the door today to get groceries, okay? It's not a big deal."

"Fine," I said, picking up a small, red toy from the floor near my foot. It had four white keys, each with a different animal. "So, you wanted to talk before I go?"

She rubbed her eyes. "Yeah."

"Where did we leave off?"

"The middle," she said.

"And how many years have we been having this particular conversation?"

"I forget."

"Four or so?"

"Something like that."

"Some variation on how you've been thinking about how much it sucks to be married to a man so much older than you who sleeps twenty out of twenty-four hours a day, although that's not really a surprise, since he's been doing that since before you were married."

"It's getting longer now," she said.

"Yes, it is, and you are wondering what kind of father he can be for Fletcher if he's always sleeping. For the thousandth time, you want advice from me, his number one pupil, on what this is all about and where it's going, because when you bring it up with him, he sidesteps the issue and makes light of it, which you take to mean he's making light of you."

She set the cup down and smiled. "Yes, but this is different. Now I've thought of a neat little solution— something new."

"Which is?" I said.

"You move in here. We can both take care of him. He's getting sicker. I could use the help. It would be a relief to have you around, even though you're a true pain in the ass sometimes."

"He's not getting sicker. There's nothing to cure."

"Healthy people don't sleep twenty hours a day."

"He's beyond health or illness."

"This again," she said.

"Your husband's not sleeping to death. He's awakening to it."

"You sound so much like him when you say irritating and confusing shit like that," she said, flipping back strands of hair. She stared into her wooden cup for a long while. "But bottom line, you're saying you won't move in?"

"Right."

"And you're saying even with the way this is accelerating, he's not really dying?" she said.

"He's overliving, if that's even a word. He's growing too substantial for the world."

She reached into an open box of animal cookies. "So, he's dying."

"Yes, in a sense."

"So, that is what you're saying."

"In a sense."

She hit her open palm on the table. "Just say it."

"Say what?"

"He's dying."

"I said 'in a sense.'"

"And in the middle of all this, in spite of the world crumbling around my four-year-old and me, you won't move in here for just a short while to help me out?"

"Help out how?"

She looked out the window. "Do I need to spell it out for you? You know what I'm saying."

"I know exactly what you're saying. I think it's a bad idea."

She stood and spilled the rest of her tea down the sink. "Fuck."

"April, come on."

"Don't," she said, holding up her hand, her back still turned. "He and I have a child who will soon be fatherless, and he'll be dead, and you're choosing this moment to maintain a safe distance. I mean, what the fuck, Lock?"

"So the solution is for you to sell me an all-access pass in return for my helping you through a situation that has you totally spooked. Fair trade: sex for protection. Oldest profession meets the second oldest."

She turned and rested her bottom against the edge of the Formica countertop, placing her palms over both eyes, whispering. "That is not what this is, and you know it."

"Right."

"Stop. I'm not just scared, Lock. I'm terrified. He's dying in little pieces. It's like some kind of magic or something is happening to him, like he's becoming a ghost. There are mornings when I can't even motivate myself to get out of bed, when I can't even emotionally put one foot in front of another. And then you say I'm being a whore."

"Sorry, that was out of line. I know that only females are allowed to have meltdowns and say all kinds of offensive shit and have it mean nothing. I'll stay quiet. Go ahead and tell me again how disappointing I am. It'll cheer you up."

She laughed, shaking her head. "You think you're funnier than you are."

"But you did smile."

"I did, but the moment has passed, buddy. Now let's get back to the part where I give you shit and you resent me for it."

"Ready, set, go."

"Okay, I know how you feel about me, and it's not just staring at my ass, cute as it is. You look at me in the way a man looks at a woman he could really be with, on all levels. Grandfather knows it too."

I stirred the tea again. "April, you are married to him. He's been my teacher for over thirty years. Now you want me to break up his marriage?"

"Pay attention. I said he and I have spoken about it. He wants me to do this. It would be a relief for him actually. He would know that I will be protected after he's gone, whenever that will be."

"You two getting a divorce?"

"Nothing so dramatic. He's just okay with this idea is all. What's holding you back?"

"How about my girlfriend, among other things?" I said.

"Pauline and you are just about over. You know it, and I know it."

"She owns the dungeon you work in, April. Don't you see the levels of shit that all this would bring for you and me?"

"I've seen how she treats you, Lock. I see how you two relate, or don't for that matter. It's not healthy."

"What do you mean you see?"

"Pauline is burnt out. She's disappointed with everyone and everything in her life. She hates running that dungeon. She looks down on you. She treats the girls with a real arrogant manner. Even the clients complain about the way she speaks to us. When we're done with a session, sometimes the clients ask me in confidence what she is PMSing about all the time. She's just negative and draining. And she's that way with you too. Is that the sort of woman you want in your life?"

"You want honesty? We're being honest right?"

"Go for it," she said.

"You have always had this competition thing with her, ever since I've known the two of you. You know how vulnerable I am when it comes to Grandfather's situation, and you're unfairly using it as a wedge. You're fighting dirty. You want to win by any means necessary. Tell me that's not part of this."

"Tell me you don't want me."

"Of course I want you. Who wouldn't want you?"

"Exactly."

"You know what?" I said, standing. "I've got to go."

"Whatever, but before you do—"

"I know. The monk."

"Just judo him or something."

"You know that's not a verb."

"What?"

"Why don't you simply call the cops?"

"Because your mentor, when he is awake, says it would be disrespectful." She set the cup down and walked out of the room. "I'm going to take a bath."

The monks' appearance had coincided with an increase in Grandfather's sleeping episodes. I recognized this one. I knelt on the grass next to him. "Can you move, please?" I said.

The sun was behind me. The man squinted. "You are his main pupil?" he replied with a slightly British accent.

"You can't just plant yourself here and chant all day. It's a residential neighborhood."

"But you are his main pupil, yes?"

"Yes."

"We trained together years ago," he said.

"Actually," I said, "I remember seeing you in Hawaii at Kauai Island, at the Hongwanji Mission."

At Janice's funeral.

"Yes."

"What is your name?" I said.

"Franklyn."

"Have you spoken with Grandfather?"

"Has he appointed you as the successor to take over the System?" Franklyn said.

"He's not appointed anyone as a successor yet."

"When he does, will it be you?"

"It's up to him," I said.

"Are you capable of teaching the System?"

"Again, it's up to him to decide that. I have to go, and so do you."

He bent down and plucked his incense sticks out of the grass. "You should prepare yourself."

CHAPTER THREE

I arrived at the Fort Lee Police Department with the de rigueur bag of donuts. The desk sergeant took two and told me Lt. Attia was on the phone.

Susan Heung's fiancé, Henry Cho, and I had originally worked together as Sam Attia's police detectives. We had both retired at the same time and opened a joint private detective agency and separate martial arts schools.

The private detective work was feast or famine, and the karate schools were break-even at best. To maintain cash flow, we had taken on a few steady bodyguarding assignments.

The largest account had been Susan Heung, whose family owned a dozen industrial parks in Bergen County. The real estate was used to launder money generated by the Heung's countywide drug distribution business. Years later, after staking his unsuccessful first run for Congress, Susan Heung became Cho's fiancée. Soon, the campaigning would begin again.

By now, in every possible way that mattered, Cho had left me behind. He had closed his karate school, moving his students to mine. He had also transferred all his bodyguarding accounts to me, including, most notably, Susan Heung and her entourage, of which he was now a part.

His second try for Congress was his current focus. Jason Heung's murder was clearly a hindrance to that goal. It was why I was reaching out to Attia without his involvement.

⁂

They left me in the waiting area for nearly half an hour. Finally, Lt. Attia's right-hand woman, Detective Sergeant Lorraine Chrysocolla, led me to his office. She waddled a bit, leading with her abdomen, as it were. Word around the station was that one of the other cops had been the half-conscious donor into her female life mate's hand at the annual Christmas party. From small beginnings...

"So, Lock, how's the dirty blonde with the muscles?" she said as we walked down the corridor.

"Her name is Pauline," I replied. "Not that it's any of your business, but we're having issues."

"Your lack of charm?"

"Could be."

"Maybe I'll give her a call."

"In your condition?"

"You see what's happening to my boobs?" she said, peeking into Attia's office. She motioned me to take a seat in the hallway. "He'll be a minute."

"No rush."

She gripped the back of the bench and eased herself into a seated position next to me. "Haven't seen you up here. You still investigating criminals or just bodyguarding them?"

"I'm here about a murder from last night."

"Boss's brother?"

"Yeah."

"A lowlife drug distributor gets killed in prison and his sister, your bodyguarding client, who is into all kinds of other illegal shit, hires you to find his killer."

"The arc of the moral universe is long, but it bends toward paying my rent."

"And protecting assholes."

"Hey, Lorraine, you want to know why the Heungs hired Cho and me to bodyguard them in the first place? Because they kept getting shaken down by cops. Evidence kept getting planted on their people. Believe it or not, Cousin Bodacious actually owns some of your colleagues in this very building."

"Vacation homes on Long Beach Island are expensive," she said.

"My point is that Susan Heung needs my protection mostly from corrupt law enforcement."

"So, you're protecting the criminals from the crooked cops. You're actually a bad guy who's a good guy."

"To be fair, I also protect the Heungs from getting shot by Cousin Bodacious."

She stroked her abdomen. "Pretty twisted shit, huh?"

"But I'm not one of them. Don't ever make that assumption."

"You got it, chief." She looked in Lt. Attia's office again. "Come on, he's finishing up."

I entered Sam's office. He was still on the phone, but motioned me to sit.

Attia was a squat, solid man in his middle fifties. He hung up. "Quickly," he said.

"I assume you heard what happened last night to Jason Heung?"

"Vaguely aware of it."

"I have a theory of who killed him," I said.

"I'm listening."

"You're behind the whole thing."

He rested his chin on his clasped hands. "Anything else?"

"Cho wanted me to ask if there was anything you could do to assist us on this."

"Assist who on what?"

"Me finding his killer," I said.

"East Jersey prison is the Bureau of Corrections. I have no authority there. And you certainly don't."

"Thanks. Can I have the real answer now?"

He leaned forward. "I'll say it slowly so you can process it audiologically. This is strictly a Corrections matter."

"You mean Cousin Bodacious's private security detail, publically known as Rahway Prison or East Jersey Prison or whatever they're calling it now, is handling the investigation in which Cousin Bodacious is the prime suspect."

"Essentially," he said.

"And that's your answer?"

"Cousin Bodacious killed Jason Heung, who was informing for me, by sheer coincidence, on Cousin Bodacious, among others. A crook was killed by a crook. You care and his sister cares. But no one else gives a shit. If you can find me another informant on Bodacious, let me know. Otherwise, leave the donuts on your way out."

"Come on, Sam."

"Come on, what?"

"Help me."

He wrote something on a piece of paper and handed it to me. "You're going to get DNA done, right?"

"Sure."

"I can give you the name of the guy we use. I'll call and let him know to expedite your sample. That's it. Happy?"

"Thanks, and the acting warden, what's his name?"

"Lt. Bergenweld," Attia said.

"Yeah, Bergenweld probably will conclude in his investigation report that an unknown fellow prisoner was involved, but there is not enough evidence to indict. Case closed; all done. Bodacious moves on to his next murder."

"Closing cases is a good thing. Keeps the wheels of justice turning."

"I guarantee Susan won't accept it," I said.

"She would be stupid if she did."

"Sam, can you do anything else?"

He leaned back and closed his eyes. "Why are you breaking my balls?"

"Come on, Sam."

"You know the drill. It's a jurisdictional issue. There's nothing I can do."

"He was your informant. That gives you jurisdiction."

"Not really."

"Come on."

"Look," he said. "If you stumble onto anything solid, keep me in the loop for informational purposes. Based upon whatever you find, I may be able to do some things quietly."

"That's all I ask."

"Now leave."

❧

Rahway Prison, a.k.a. East Jersey State Prison, had its own morgue. It was deep below ground. There were three refrigerated body storage drawers. Two of them were empty. The third had been pulled completely out.

The technician motioned Susan Heung and me to approach. I followed her. Lt. Bergenweld was off to the side, arms crossed, leaning against a stack of boxes labeled Formaldehyde.

All I recognized was Jason's characteristic nose ring; it was the only part of him that had made it through the fire intact. I had always assumed prisoners were not allowed to wear jewelry. Apparently, Jason was an exception.

Susan showed no reaction. "How did this happen?" she said.

"It's under investigation," Lt. Bergenweld replied.

"Who found him?" I said.

"Sergeant Taylor."

"I want to speak to him."

"She's waiting in my conference room."

Sergeant Trudy Taylor sat at the head of the conference table with an open manila folder in front of her. She was a middle-aged African American woman whose blue prison guard uniform seemed a size too small. Her rust-colored hair was mixed with gray. She wore a few silver bangles on one wrist that kept sliding as she moved her arm.

Lt. Bergenweld sat next to her. "This meeting is being arranged as a courtesy to the family," he said. "There is an ongoing investigation, so the nature and extent of the information we can share is limited. But within those parameters, I'm willing to have Sergeant Taylor answer a few questions."

"When did you find the body?" I said.

She tilted her head up so that her reading glasses were in line with the report in front of her. "After lights out yesterday. I was on patrol of the trash area. North Wing. It's under construction."

"How did you find him?"

"There was smoke coming from one of the bins. I investigated and found a small fire had been set. The body was in there."

"What else was in there?"

"Garbage, burned mostly. That's it."

"How did you identify him?"

"The jumpsuits all have serial numbers. Also, he was the only prisoner missing last night."

I turned to Lt. Bergenweld. "You are doing an autopsy for confirmation?"

"Yes. Standard."

"The family will want to do a second one after yours."

"Not without a court order."

"We won't need a second autopsy," Susan Heung said. "We know how he died. I wish to take my brother's possessions now."

"Of course."

"I also wish to be kept apprised of the progress of the investigation," Susan said.

"Consistent with the integrity of the investigation, I have no issue with that."

"Before we go, I would at least like to take a sample of his tissue for DNA testing," I said.

"We don't generally do that with a cadaver," Bergenweld replied.

"I'll have it tested myself by an outside lab that was recommended by Lt. Attia from Fort Lee," I said.

"Fine."

❧

I drove Susan's car back to Fort Lee. She sat in the back making calls and checking email messages. Eventually, she placed her cell phone on the seat and tapped me on the shoulder. "What did Lt. Attia tell you?"

"Nothing of importance," I said. "When I mentioned that Cousin Bodacious has infiltrated the prison, he did not deny it. But we knew that."

"Yes, and a month ago, Henry and I tried to get your Lt. Attia to transfer Jason out of that prison, and that did not happen. Then, he was murdered by Bodacious's men."

"Maybe; we don't know for certain."

"And someone assumes that I will not pursue this," she said.

"I don't know what whoever did this assumes," I said.

"Do you have any suggestions?"

"I will send the tissue to a lab for DNA sampling."

"What else?"

"I can also have a talk with that prison guard, Taylor. Better for your people to find out her home address if possible, rather than have me search for it through my law enforcement contacts. Then I'll go there and see if she will speak with me."

"Will Lt. Attia help or hinder in this?"

"What he can do is limited. It's out of his jurisdiction."

"Convenient."

"What does that mean?" I said.

"You anticipate that Cousin Bodacious will react in some way if he learns you are speaking with this Taylor?" Susan said.

"I do."

"We are prepared for that?" she said.

"As much as we can be. I'll react to his reaction."

She unfolded her reading glasses and looked at her cell phone again. "Anything else?"

"At some point, I should probably go into the prison and interview Jason's former cellmate," I said, "the one who you used to pass information back and forth when you tried to cut a deal for Jason's early release."

"Can that be done?"

"Not in the way you previously did it."

"How do we reopen communications with the cellmate now?"

"Let me see what happens with Taylor first. I have an idea how she can help us. After I speak to her, I'll know better if that's doable."

"What if she informs Bergenweld?"

"There's nothing to inform about. They expect us to try to find out what happened to Jason, and the logical approach is to make contact with someone on the inside. There's no danger of disclosing something that they already expect us to do. The only real danger is to me because I'm the one who will be going in there to make contact."

Susan was silent. I looked in the rearview mirror and saw her staring out the window at a natural gas facility beyond the Turnpike guardrail.

"What?" I said.

"Arrangements are being made to bring in someone to work in tandem with your investigation. He represents the South Korean interests we do business with. I want you to cooperate with him."

"Who?"

"You have met him before. His name is Kim Jaegyu."

"Over a year ago, I bodyguarded while you met with him. I never said two words to the man."

"Now you will."

"Why are you involving him?"

"Because our friends in South Korea offered to help. To refuse would be dishonorable."

"What is this guy's background?"

"He brought us BOK. He was a middleman, so to speak. They finance our real estate holdings."

"BOK?"

"Bank of Korea."

We drove in silence. "Susan, I don't mind keeping Jaegyu informed. But I don't want him to step all over my investigation. I head your security detail. You need to let me do my job."

"I would think that you would welcome the assistance."

"Is he working for me?"

"No, the two of you will work in tandem. He is not my employee. He is a free agent."

"Why don't you tell this Jaegyu to hold off for a week or two until I do my thing? If I come up empty, you can bring him in then."

She leaned against the headrest. "You never liked my brother, did you, Lock?"

"We had words from time to time. But I never let it interfere with my obligation to bodyguard you, or on occasion, him for that matter. I think he respected that. He had a sense of honor in a twisted sense."

Susan smiled to herself. "He was also a difficult brother in a twisted sense. Our father was a difficult father in a twisted sense. My life has unfolded in a twisted sense."

"I know," I said.

"When my father came to this country, the doors were closed to Koreans. It was 1951. How many opportunities do you think Koreans had in this country during the Korean War? But Jason grew up in a different era. It was not necessary for him to live in my father's world."

"He disagreed."

"I could never convince him to transfer our family holdings to the real estate ventures exclusively."

"We'll find out who did this, Susan."

"Perhaps."

CHAPTER FOUR

After dropping Susan off, I went to my apartment above the karate school. I tried to take a nap to make up for being woken the night before but eventually gave up.

I opened the front door to let in the summer breeze. A few of our students were across the street hanging out by the candy store. They were early.

I went back inside, locked the door, and changed into my black Chinese Tai Chi Chuan uniform. The blue floor mat felt spongy against my bare feet. I centered myself, taking long slow breaths, and began the glorious Yang-style Tai Chi long form.

The movements were slow and gentle, informed by a graceful rocking akin to making love to the air. It took me nearly twenty minutes to complete the form's 108 postures—gentle waves, slower than slow.

Most people did not know that Tai Chi was also a deadly Chinese martial art. Many considered it one of the most effective of all the Kung Fu styles. When its slow and graceful movements were performed with maximum speed and power, they were practically impossible to defend against.

It had been twenty years since Grandfather had taught me this form. It was an extraordinary gift, one of many he had given me.

His time on this Earth was coming to an end. The monks making their way back and forth to his front lawn were evidence of that. A great presence was about to depart. As they had for centuries, the Eastern spiritual leaders were gathering for his Last Statement followed by a Last Celebration of his life.

I finished the Tai Chi form and made myself some green tea. I heard the key turn in the front door. Bette, my stepdaughter from my second marriage, to Janice, entered the school. She emptied a brown paper bag of oranges onto one of the parent chairs. "The afternoon kids' class will be starting soon." She locked herself in my small office to change.

"How's college?" I called out.

"Nothing to report," she said through the door.

When she came out, she was wearing her black karate uniform with the second-degree black belt Grandfather and I had awarded her the previous winter. Her auburn hair was tied in a bun. As the kids began to arrive, she lay on the mat and started stretching.

Eventually, the school filled with about twenty children in an assortment of white, yellow, and green belts practicing with Bette how to push away an attacker. It was the least violent of our self-defense techniques, one particularly suited to a child being attacked by a larger bully: simply push and run.

The kids were paired off. They would take turns pushing one another onto a soft pad we had set up on the edge of the mat. The parents sat on plastic chairs on the other side of the room by the doorway.

About halfway through the class, Bette told the kids to gather around her in a semicircle. "You're not using the rule we discussed," she said. "You are all just pushing the other person away. That won't give you the time to run. It's like pushing a small tree. It just bounces back at you." She motioned me to approach. "Sifu Tourmaline has volunteered to be one of the bad guys."

"Are you going to be gentle with me?" I said.

"Sure," she said, making a face to the children. They giggled.

Bette placed her hands on my chest. I was a head taller than her and at least sixty pounds heavier. She pushed, and I took one step back. "You see?" she said. "That was as hard as I could push, but he's bigger than me, so it didn't do anything. What would be a better way of pushing? How can I move a tree so it doesn't just bounce back?"

One of the kids raised her hand. "Cut it down?"

Bette tapped the instep of her foot a few times against my ankle. "Yes, we could sweep him here. If we do it at the right angle and with the right force, and we pull his shoulder back as we kick his ankle out, that might get him to fall. Shall we try?"

I held up my hands and said to the kids, "What did she just say?"

Suddenly, Bette swiveled her right hip inward, whipping her right foot just under my calf. Her right hand grabbed the shoulder of my T-shirt and yanked it backward. Immediately, my leg shot out from under me, and I landed on my back.

She went with me to the ground, hooking the back of my leg with her left arm and pressing it toward my chest. She snaked her other hand behind my head and interlaced her fingers, pulling me into a tight ball.

The kids clapped.

She released me, and I gradually stood again.

"But that is a lot to remember," she said. "And it hurts the person, especially if you throw them to the pavement. I am looking for an easy and gentle way of pushing away a bully. How can we do it gently?"

The same girl raised her hand. "Ask him to leave you alone?"

"Yes, but what if he doesn't leave you alone?"

They were silent.

"The answer is that we uproot the tree first and then we push. Once it is uprooted, we can throw it as far as we want. Kicking his ankle is cutting the tree with a saw. We want to gently uproot it and toss it away. Watch."

Bette placed her fingertips on my chest. She twisted her feet inward, transferring her inner *chi* energy up her legs, bending her knees in an undulating curve. The wave traveled whip-like up her body, through her abdomen and chest and down her shoulders. Her elbows curved around, and the movement terminated at her palms. At just that moment, her knees, hips, and elbows straightened upward.

For an instant, I was lifted off the ground. She immediately shuffled one step forward into my center and exhaled audibly, pushing into me with a short but sudden, explosive thrust of her forearm buttressed by the palm of her other hand, what the Chinese call *Jing*.

My body arced into the air and landed about six feet away. I curled into a ball and rolled backward, terminating the movement in a standing position.

The kids laughed and clapped, as did some of the parents.

"A little person like me can do that," Bette said. "Any of you can do it too. Want to try?"

"But not on me, again," I said. More giggles.

The kids paired off to practice. Bette stepped off the mat with me. She tossed an orange in my direction and whispered, "Isn't that April out front?"

"So it is," I said. "You okay here?"

"Go talk to her," she said.

I smiled. "You're very pushy today."

I walked past a bunch of parents bobbing and weaving to get a better look at their kids. When I reached the small vestibule, I gave April a hug and said, "Come into my office."

"Before you ask, Grandfather's up," she said, as we both entered the small room. "I left him showering."

"So, the acupuncture worked," I said, tossing her the orange Bette had given me.

"Until the next time. I've decided to put it out of my mind today. I'm taking a vacation from the lunacy."

"Good idea."

"I stopped by for a different reason. How's the Jason Heung investigation going?"

"It's going."

"And you're still liking Cousin Bodacious for this?" she said.

"More or less," I said.

"Don't you have contacts with his organization?"

"Yes, I do."

"Len LeFontant, right?" she said. "He's the head of Bodacious's security. He was a police detective too. You're friends."

"He was a detective in Fair Lawn. Both Bodacious and the Heungs like to have retired detectives on their payroll. How do you know him?"

"Comes around the dungeon to collect money for Bodacious. Grabs my ass. Hates women."

"You get a lot of that."

"You have no idea," she said. "So, why not just speak to Len?"

"Eventually, I will."

"How about sooner than that?"

"Where is this heading, April?"

"I was thinking that since I'm seeing him anyway tomorrow, you might come along."

"You're seeing Len LeFontant tomorrow?"

"Yeah."

"Why would you be seeing Cousin Bodacious's head of security?"

"I'm doing a session with him."

"A session at the dungeon?"

"At his beach house in Elberon. I thought maybe you might come down and speak to him after we conduct our business."

"What possible upside could there be for you to do a session freelance with the head of Cousin Bodacious's security detail?"

"Trying to solve a problem."

"What kind of problem?"

"A Lori problem."

"Jesus."

"You remember the muscle builder Lori was dating a few years ago, the guy who got murdered?"

"Tom; I was there when he was murdered."

"Apparently, he shot a sex tape with her. Len has it. She needs to get it back."

"And Bodacious is selling it?"

"Bodacious's people are selling it as part of a horny ex-girlfriends series on DVD. They have a warehouse full of porno they distribute. It's off Market Street in Newark, near the Court House."

"I know the warehouse address. How did they get the video?"

"No idea. Maybe Tom needed money."

"That guy was always trouble."

"Lori's taste in men," she said.

"Funny."

"In other words, she's your first wife and proceeds to divorce you and then ends up with him. Her taste in men is questionable. That's the joke."

"I get it, right. I'm laughing, but on the inside where you can't see. Why are you involving yourself in this?"

"She's my best friend."

"Lori is your best friend? My Lori?" I said.

"Be nice. You're the one who introduced us. I'm going to help her. This DVD is something from years ago. Tom's dead, and she's not a wild child anymore. She's trying to start a new life and put this sort of craziness behind her. But in the digital age you can't just put things behind you, right? Nothing ever just goes away once it gets on the Internet, which by the way it has not yet, though it no doubt eventually will."

"You writing an article?"

"I want to help her. It would be nice if you helped her too. She won't ask directly, but you should."

"So bottom line is that you're here to volunteer me for the latest Lori crisis. Thanks, I'll pass."

"Are you saying you've given up protecting women who have contempt for you? I thought it was your lifelong passion."

"Taking a short break."

"Okay, break's over."

"April."

"You know you're going to say yes in the end. Why dance around it?"

I paused. "How are you involved in this again?"

"Lori got Len to agree that he would sell her back the DVDs and keep the digital files off the Internet if she paid double cost and if she threw a session with me into the deal on a freelance basis."

"You and Len?"

"He has his hands all over me when he visits the dungeon. I respond by saying something insulting, which just turns him on even more. I think he wants to put me in my place."

"And does Pauline, who happens to be my girlfriend and your boss at the dungeon, know you're freelancing behind her back?"

"No."

"And you know Pauline doesn't allow freelance."

"Yes."

"But are you going to tell her?"

"No, and neither will you."

"Jesus, April."

"Don't strain your brain on this."

I stared at the sidewalk through my office's plate glass window. A German shepherd was leashed to a parking meter near the candy store. "And just to fill in the rest of the blanks, you need me there why?"

"Just in case things get out of hand."

"So, you'll be the talent and I'll be the muscle."

"You're the dungeon's bouncer. So, just bounce your way down to Elberon with Lori and me, and everything will be fine."

"You know Len's a maniac when it comes to females, a major lunatic."

"Like you aren't? I've been throwing myself at you, and you still don't get that I'm ready, willing, and able to rock your world. What kind of lunatic does that make you?"

"April, you know this is a bad idea, even by Lori standards. Really, really bad."

"Absolutely—a very, very bad idea. So you'll do it?"

The dog was chewing on its leash and growling. "You're right about one thing," I said. "It is too dangerous for you two to go alone."

"So that's a yes?"

"If I refuse, you'll make a face, and I'll do it anyway."

"It's so much easier when you just obey the females in your life."

CHAPTER FIVE

Late that night, I parked my car across from the Rahway Prison parking lot and waited for Sergeant Trudy Taylor to end her shift. Since our afternoon meeting, Susan's contacts had developed a detailed dossier on Taylor, which she had emailed to me. I opened it on my cell phone while I waited to see if there was anything I could use.

Taylor had been a corrections officer for fourteen years. She had made sergeant after seven. Before joining the prison unit, she had been a laid-off elementary school teacher. She had grown up near Newark in East Orange and only moved to Red Bank after her divorce.

She was thirty-eight, African American, and a smoker. She frequented the local taverns in Red Bank, where she played in a local girl band. She had three disciplinary letters in her file. Two were for coming to work late and the third for insubordination. The last letter had been signed by Lt. Bergenweld. It apparently involved an assignment he had given her that she had refused to carry out.

I unscrewed my brushed-metal thermos bottle and took a sip of decaf coffee. Just as I returned it under the driver's seat, her car pulled out from the lot.

I followed her south to Red Bank. Since I knew her address, I was able to veer away when we both took Exit 109 off the Garden State Parkway. I circled around and parked two blocks from her apartment building. I jogged back and acquired her just as she was coming out of her car.

She was wearing her prison guard uniform and carrying a duffel bag with the acronym, EJSP.

She turned and pointed her Taser at me. "Halt."

"You won't need that," I said. "I'll protect you from any ruffians that may be about."

"You're from this morning," she said.

"I have a few questions."

"You asked me your questions."

"I have more."

She put the Taser away. "What if I don't want to answer?"

"You and I both know who very likely killed Jason Heung."

"I know who your boss believes killed Jason Heung," she said.

"I want to nail that down, either pro or con," I said. "Does that interest you?"

She crossed her arms. "Don't you think that might be a conflict of interest, being that his sister is also a suspect?"

"You think Susan Heung killed her own brother?"

"Why not? He was informing to the police about what he knew. The thing he knew the most about was his own family's business dealings."

"He was informing on Cousin Bodacious."

"He's a suspect too," she said.

"He should be your prime suspect. Susan had no way of getting to Jason. Bodacious owns that prison. You of all people know that. You work there."

"We'll see."

"So, let me ask you this," I said. "If you find that Cousin Bodacious ordered Jason Heung killed, you will make that conclusion in your report?"

"Absolutely."

"And you'll submit that to Lt. Bergenweld?"

"Yes."

"And what do you think he'll do with it?"

"Not my concern."

"He'll shred it."

"Again, not my concern."

"So, you'd be okay with the killer going free?"

"What do you want from me?"

"Get me in the prison."

"Why?"

"I want to do my own digging."

"Digging how?"

"Just get me in and get me out."

"Why should I?"

"Because you want to find out who killed Jason Heung. So do I. You have my word that I will share the evidence I gather. Essentially, I'll be doing your job."

"And if what you give me is total bullshit?"

"Even that would help you. If I give you bullshit, it just increases the likelihood that my boss is hiding something. That is what law enforcement types sometimes call a clue."

"Assuming I go along with this, how do you propose I get you in?"

"Undercover as a prisoner or a guard."

"And of course, the next thing you're going to tell me is that I can't let Lt. Bergenweld in on our little plan."

"That's right."

"How do you know I'm not co-opted by Cousin Bodacious too? How do you know that I'm not going to call Bergenweld and let him know about our little conversation?"

"Doesn't matter. Even if you do, what are you going to tell him? That Susan Heung's people are investigating Jason Heung's murder? How is that news? He knows already."

"I might tell him that you're going undercover in the prison. It might put you in a small bit of danger, don't you think?"

"Calculated risk."

"Reckless stupidity."

"Not the first time."

"So, I'm going to give you an orange jumpsuit or a blue uniform and you think you'll be able to just wander around wherever you want to, and no one will stop you? You think that's how prison works?"

"Leave that to me. Will you at least consider it?"

"I'll consider it."

"I'll be in touch."

❧

The next morning I drove to Susan Heung's penthouse office in the Winston Towers complex in Cliffside Park. It had once been her father's. After his murder, Jason had moved in. Once Jason was incarcerated, Susan had left her two-story, white stucco office building on the other side of Route 67 and done the same.

I took the dedicated elevator to the top floor. The reception area was massive. The sole illumination was the pinpoint recessed track lighting shining upon the dozen or so original Jackson Pollocks that had been in her father's collection.

I entered Susan's office. Cho was sitting on the couch, eating a hoagie. From the writing on the bag, I knew he had picked it up from the Fort Lee Diner. It had been his favorite place to eat since the days when we had been detectives together. Upon his ascension to borough councilman and future congressman, they had named the hoagie after him: the Henry Cho Special.

Susan was in her chair behind the granite-topped desk. She had to step on a platform to get there. Originally, it had been built in that manner to raise her father's five-foot frame above the rest of the room.

"Hey, Lock, we were talking about last-minute wedding stuff," Cho said over a mouthful of sandwich. "Glad you interrupted."

"Aren't you supposed to be in Washington vetting a new campaign manager?" I said.

"Decided to stick around for a while."

Susan pointed behind me. "Say hello to Kim Jaegyu."

He was a tall Korean man in his forties. He wore a charcoal gray, pinstripe suit with a silk, burgundy handkerchief in the breast pocket.

I shook his hand. He just stared at me.

"An update, please," Susan said.

"In private?" I said.

"This is fine."

"I met with the prison officer who found the body. I think the way to get information from her is to give it, as well. It has to be reciprocal."

"What information do we have to give her?" Susan said.

"Nothing yet."

"You're going to go in undercover to meet with the cellmate?"

I looked at Jaegyu. He stared back. "Susan, let's not discuss this now," I said.

"What do you need?"

"Money, probably," I said.

"How much?"

"I'll let you know."

"And she'll get you inside the prison?" Susan said.

"Can we put off this discussion for now?"

"Take Mr. Jaegyu when you see her next."

"That's a bad idea, Susan."

"It's a very good idea," Jaegyu said from the back of the room. He was leaning against the wall, brushing his hand along the sleeve of his suit.

"And another thing," Susan said. "What if Lt. Attia was complicit in arranging the circumstances of the attack on my brother?"

"Again with this?" I said.

"Just answer her question," Jaegyu said.

"Has he been filling your head with this nonsense?" I said to Susan.

"Mr. Jaegyu is doing his job," she said. "Answer me."

"Sam Attia had nothing to do with killing your brother."

"He may have concluded that my brother violated the condition of cooperation," she said.

"Just because the cooperation went nowhere is not a reason to kill someone."

"Maybe there is more to it."

"Not with Sam Attia," I said.

Cho wiped his mouth and took a swig of Diet Coke. "Susan, I served under Sam Attia too. That's not him."

She kept her gaze fixed on her hands. "You and Lock served under him over six years ago. People change; circumstances change."

"Not to that extent," I said.

"So, you are ruling him out as a suspect?" Jaegyu said.

I turned to him. "And just how are you going to investigate him as a suspect? You going to go down to the Police Department and ask around?"

"Not him; you," Susan said. "You will investigate all possible leads, including Sam Attia."

"In other words, you will assist me," Jaegyu said.

I turned back to Susan. "I thought I didn't report to this guy."

"You report to me," Susan said, "and I am telling you to pursue all leads."

"This is bullshit," I said.

"Why did Lt. Attia not have Jason Heung transferred out of that facility, knowing that Cousin Bodacious owned it?" Jaegyu said.

"You don't understand American law enforcement," I said. "There was no control on Attia's part in that prison. He's a Fort Lee detective lieutenant and head of the Organized Crime Strike Force. The prisons are separate from the police. This isn't Seoul."

"Lock," Susan said. Her eyes were blank. I had seen that look before. "My brother was killed in that prison. We need redress. You will have the money and anything else you request. But understand that it needs to be pursued wherever it may lead. I trust that will happen."

"Are you implying something, Susan?"

"You work for me. If I did not trust you to do your job, you would not be in that position."

"Attia should not be on the list," I said.

She paused. "He will remain on the list until I am convinced he should be removed."

CHAPTER SIX

That night, Pauline and I had an early dinner. I stayed at her place and woke the next morning to an empty bed. I put on my robe and went downstairs.

She was in the middle of her living room, lifting thirty-pound dumbbells. The room had a vaulted ceiling and two skylights. The sun was in a direct line with her face, causing her to squint.

Everything about the house was oversized. She called it her McMansion, one of many in Englewood Cliffs. Running a cash dungeon had its perks.

She was on her back working the pecs. I waited until her arms were completely spread open, leaned down and kissed her. After a moment, she whispered, "I'm gonna drop these."

I broke off the kiss, and she resumed the repetitions. "You had breakfast?" I said.

"There's some whole-wheat toast left for you."

I went to the kitchen, took the slices and poured myself orange juice.

Pauline and I had met years ago when I was a police detective. I had served a summons on her based upon a neighbor's harassment complaint that implied she was running a house of prostitution. While waiting for her court case to be called, we had gotten to talking. It became obvious that she was actually running a no-sex-allowed,

BDSM dungeon called *Strapped by the Lash* and that it was perfectly legal.

I asked the prosecutor to drop the charges. That led to Pauline enrolling her little girl in the karate school and offering me off-duty work as a bouncer. That led to me suggesting she hire Grandfather to fill in when I was not available. That led Grandfather to April.

I rejoined her in the living room. I sat on the leather couch and propped my bare feet on the coffee table. "Bette told me Shayna is testing for her brown belt," I said, biting into the toast.

"Yes, and do you realize the shit that's going to come down if you and Bette fail her?"

"She'll do fine."

Pauline wiped her face with a pink towel. "Actually, Bette seems to be doing a terrific job teaching the karate classes. In fact, I was thinking of offering her a slot at the dungeon. I have a long list of men who would just love to be uprooted and pushed across the room."

"Don't even joke about that."

She folded the towel and placed it on the bench. "I need to ask you something."

"No, I cannot give you more sex," I said. "I've reached the human limit."

"Your ex-wife has made some kind of unholy alliance with April. You know anything about that?"

"You have to ask April."

"I asked April. Got nothing."

"Ask her again."

Pauline sat next to me and stroked my ear. "Come on, I know you're lying. Tell me."

"Nothing to tell."

She leaned her head into the crook of my shoulder. "And one more thing, Mr. Lock Tourmaline, why do you look so sad all the time? What is that about?"

"Grandfather," I said.

"Is it getting close?"

"Very."

She kissed me and rested her head on my chest. "Four years ago you went through it with your second wife and now this."

"The difference is Janice had cancer. Grandfather is voluntarily shuffling off this mortal coil."

"Kind of makes it worse."

"Yeah."

"And that call a couple of nights ago about Jason Heung. You working for Susan Heung on that?"

"Yeah."

"I thought we agreed you were going to disengage from the Heungs. You don't belong with them."

"We agreed that I would slowly disengage. I'm doing that."

"By investigating Jason's murder?"

"I can't just pull out suddenly. I rely on the bodyguarding for most of my revenue, not the karate school, not following boyfriends or girlfriends that are suspected of cheating, not my meager police pension. Without the Heungs, I am in serious red ink."

"So, you're stuck."

"For now. And believe me, if I don't solve this murder, she'll dump me anyway."

"So, solve the murder and get this over with."

"Solving the murder is about proving who did it. Everyone assumes Bodacious had someone do it. Even if it's as simple as that, there will be no evidence, no witnesses. And even if there were, who would arrest Bodacious? Who would prosecute him? He's beyond local law enforcement, has been for years. This will not end well."

"So, what's the plan?"

"Play it out and hope something breaks my way. People make mistakes. Shit happens. I just need to keep going and hope for the best."

"Some plan."

"What about you?" I said.

"I'm having the same nervous breakdown I've been talking about for the last year," she said. "I'm bored of talking about it in fact."

"Is there anything I can do to help?" I said.

"You can stop lying to me."

"Besides that."

"You can get me out of this dopey business I'm running. You can get me away from the girls who undermine my authority, number one being your April, and the cat fights I need to break up, and the clients who slobber over and grope everything in black patent leather boots and a garter belt, and your pal, Cousin Bodacious, who doesn't believe in the words recession or cash flow problem but insists on getting his ten percent every month like clockwork. I've boxed myself into a corner with this thing. When I was younger, it seemed like a lark and a cash cow, a feminist empowerment thing, taking control of fetishistic sexuality without the actual sex and doing it with a feminine twist, without being abusive to the women, strictly on my terms, and getting paid to boot. Now, it's becoming something darker, something smothering."

"I know."

She took a deep breath. "And to top it all off, no matter how hard I try, I can't be your dead wife. It pisses me off as much as it does you."

"I know that too," I said.

She ran her fingers through my hair. "We should really break up, you know. It would be much healthier for both of us."

"We're too self-destructive to do something that healthy," I said

"So we stick it out?"

"No, we break up, but we do it in the most self-destructive way possible."

"Something to look forward to," she said, gathering up the pink towel. "Anyway, I'm late to the dungeon. Clean the dishes, okay?"

"My purpose in life."

❦

I arrived at the law firm where my ex-wife, Lori, worked. It was located in a dark glass building in Fort Lee, overlooking the massive set of tollbooths on the Jersey Side of the George Washington Bridge.

The firm was situated on one of the lower floors. The receptionist told me that Lori was out to lunch but would be returning soon.

I read one of the brochures laid out on the coffee table. It had pictures of twelve lawyers. I picked out Lori's fiancé. His name was Lloyd Garrison, and the brochure said he practiced something called transactional law.

Eventually, Lori and Lloyd returned from lunch. She was wearing a light blue pants suit. Her blond hair was closely cropped. Her face tightened when she saw me. "I said I would meet you downstairs."

"Hi, Lori," I replied.

"I'm Lloyd," her boyfriend said, shaking my hand. "Please to meet you." His right eye drooped slightly. It was hard to tell how badly since he wore tinted glasses. He had brown hair and was wearing a polo shirt with light gray slacks.

"Likewise," I said. "And congratulations on the engagement."

"You know you'll be invited to the wedding. From what she's told me, you're still a big part of Lori's life. I'd like that to continue."

"And on that note," Lori said, kissing Lloyd on the cheek. "I'm taking my personal half day as of now. See you tomorrow."

"Bye, Lloyd," I said.

"Good-bye, Lock."

"Let's go," Lori said. As we approached the elevator, she whispered to me, "I could tell the asshole in you was about to come out."

⌘

Pauline's dungeon, *Strapped by the Lash*, was located in a nondescript building in a residential neighborhood on 81st Street just off Kennedy Boulevard in North Bergen. Lori and I parked a few blocks away. We waited for April to join us. Her shift had just ended.

"You know, Lori," I said. "The guy you're negotiating with is affiliated with Bodacious at a pretty high level."

"So?" she said. "Does it surprise you that a criminal distributes pornography?"

"That's not the point. I know this Len LeFontant really well. He is jacked in directly to Bodacious. And pornography distribution is certainly not one of the main Bodacious operations. It's actually died out because of free Internet distribution channels. That's probably why he has a warehouse full of this stuff. It doesn't sell anymore."

"Again, so?"

"The so is that I wish you had come to me first," I said. "I might have been able to speak to him or some of my other contacts among Bodacious's people to get this done more quietly. One of my jobs for Susan is to function as a liaison on behalf of the Heung interests vis-à-vis the Bodacious interests. They each run their street drug businesses in adjoining counties, Bodacious in Essex and Hudson and the Heungs in Bergen. At least the Heungs used to run Bergen. Susan's reduced the family's involvement dramatically. But there are still a lot of small disputes that arise. Len and I work them out quietly."

"Spare me."

"No really, Lori, Bodacious and the Heungs are competitors of a sort, but they also have to coexist. So, there is a loose network of former cops that work for people like this to help them do that. We don't get involved in anything illegal—at least I don't. But we try to smooth ruffled feathers if we can. My point is that I could have approached Len a little more subtly."

"You're a former cop who works for the people you used to arrest. You're a sellout and a hypocrite. Nothing about you is subtle."

"That certainly is another way of looking at it."

"I mean, honestly, this is just about retrieving one of a thousand sick titles this guy distributes. What does he care? Is he going to run out of pornography because he gives me back my fifteen minutes of film? This is very minor for him. And I have money to pay. What is the big deal?"

"What I was trying to tell you is that the porn industry has completely changed. DVDs like this are not the current means of distribution. You're right in that I cannot believe Bodacious really cares about giving back his entire stock of one of these titles for a good price, but I could have worked something out under the table, quietly."

"Like that would really happen."

"What are you talking about?"

"I knew if I came to you and told you someone has pictures of me fucking, you'd just laugh it up behind my back. Once again, I'd be the clown."

"Jesus," I said. I turned on the car radio and flipped through five stations. They were all playing commercials. "By the way, where are you getting the money to buy out the stock of DVDs, your fiancé?"

"Lloyd doesn't know about it, okay? I'm paying it from savings. It's all the money I have from that bag they left after Tom's murder, remember?"

"I was there."

"I know you were there." Tears formed at the corner of her eyes. "Don't pick on me, okay? I'm incredibly embarrassed by all this. Can't you see that? I did some stupid things that I can't erase, one of which was marrying you, by the way. Another was shooting this tape with Tom, the asshole boyfriend who beat me—"

"I remember."

"So, I've been trying hard to put all these toxic relationships behind me. But the film is out there, and so I really can't put it behind me, now can I? I can't move on with this hanging over my head. What if I have a girl someday, and she sees her mother on a video like this? Or Jesus Christ, a boy? You think I want anyone, you think I want you, watching me give head?"

I looked in my rearview mirror. April was walking toward us. "Which brings up another question, how did you find out about this anyway?" I said.

"I was in a store with Lloyd and I saw my face on a DVD cover. I was able to usher us out of there before he saw it too."

"What were you and Lloyd doing in one of those stores?"

She wiped her eyes with a tissue. "Just for two seconds, could you stop being such an asshole?"

April tapped on my window. She was holding two plastic milk crates, leaning back to balance them on her thigh. Through their grills, I could see an assortment of colored ropes, leather handcuffs, massage oil, and all manner of crops and soft, rubber whips. A clear plastic garment bag was draped on top.

I got out of the car. "How's Grandfather this morning?" I said.

"He was up when I left, played with Fletcher for a while, did his Judo exercises."

"Not Judo, we don't do Judo. Stop saying Judo. I've never learned one lesson of Judo and neither has he. What we do is Shaolin Kempo Karate and Tai Chi and Qi Gong and Plumb Blossom Kung Fu."

"Lori bringing out the PMS in you?"

"It's just you always say it's Judo. It's not Judo."

"You want a Motrin?"

"This is going to be a long day, isn't it?" I said.

"Think of what I have to do. Want to trade places?"

"Not really."

"Help me with this. It's heavy."

I took the crates from her. "Sorry," I said, "Lori put me in a bad mood. Let's just get this done."

April nudged me with her hip. "There's the Lock Tourmaline I remember. Back to helping women who have contempt for him. Sure you still remember how to do it?"

"Like riding a bicycle."

CHAPTER SEVEN

*April sat next to me in the front of the car. She was wearing stone-*washed jeans and an oversized white T-shirt. Lori lay across the back seat, reading a paralegal training manual.

My side view of the highway was partially obscured by April's transparent garment bag hanging from the handhold above the back passenger door. It contained the uniform of the day: vinyl black miniskirt, fishnet hosiery, and fuck-me stiletto pumps. She also had two zipper bags hooked to the larger one. They were filled with cosmetics—what she called war paint.

I found Len's address on my GPS's previous destination list. I had been to his beach house last month for a fundraiser. It had to do with a scholarship program for young minorities who had been through one of Cousin Bodacious's Newark drug rehab centers.

The Garden State Parkway was heavily trafficked. As we slowed to a crawl, April propped her elbows just under the headrest, twisting her body to speak to Lori in the back seat. "Hello, dear, what's that?"

"Homework for a course I'm taking," Lori said.

"You want me to have Daddy buy us ice cream?"

Lori placed a finger down her throat.

April turned back and took the makeup compact from her purse to redo her lipstick. "How did you put her in such a foul mood?"

"My skill-set."

❧

The house was located on an acre of secluded beach front. It was adorned with an abundance of green foliage punctuated by a small, artificial stream. The last time I was here, Len had shown me a petition his neighbors had left on his doorstep asking him to kindly consider moving because of Cousin Bodacious' illicit activities. In response, he had placed a statue of an African American man dressed in a jockey outfit and holding a lantern. He said it was his way of shouting out a big fuck you to his "racist neighbors."

A middle-aged Hispanic woman was sitting on a marble garden bench. She wore a blue maid's uniform. I distantly remembered her as one of the servers from the fundraiser.

I parked on the crushed gravel driveway and joined her. The name tag read, Aida. "We're here to see Mr. LeFontant," I said.

"I should tell you for the young lady to change in the guest cabana," she said.

I lifted one of the two milk crates out of the trunk. April took the garment bag and cosmetic kit. We walked to the cabana. There were brightly colored fish painted along the top and bottom of its outside wall. She closed the blue, louvered door behind her.

"Miss," Aida called into the cabana. "I was told by Mr. please do not go outside in your outfit for the neighbors. Come in the other door along the path."

"Fine, yes, okay," I heard April call from inside.

Aida guided Lori and me into the main foyer of the beach house. Shortly thereafter, April joined us. She was dressed in the tight-fitting, black miniskirt and pumps. Her footsteps made a loud clacking sound on the white marble floor.

I pointed where I had set down the milk crates. She squatted to take out her equipment. I unconsciously looked away. *Feminine candlepower.*

"Where is he?" April said, swinging the riding crop in front of her. It made a whistling sound.

"Upstairs, waiting for Miss," Aida said.

"Hold on," Lori said. "Where's the DVD inventory? We can start loading it into the car while you're up there."

"I just to send the lady upstairs," Aida said.

"Relax," April said. "I'll talk to him after the session. I promise. He'll be more malleable."

"Whatever," Lori said.

The maid directed Lori and me to a wooden deck on the side of the house overlooking the ocean. The sun reflected a jagged line off the water. The sky had a light reddish hue behind the scud clouds. It would rain tomorrow.

We sat there in silence. I glanced at the second-floor window of Len's house and rubbed my lower back, stretching. There were seagulls making mad Kamikaze runs at the shoreline, squawking at one another.

She crossed her arms. "I'm cold."

"You know, I am really happy you have that job. It looks like an interesting place to work."

Some strands of hair fell across her forehead. "It's a job."

"You work directly for Lloyd?"

"Yeah."

"He seems nice."

"Actually, he's everything you always looked down on, someone sitting in an office pushing paper. I know how you feel about people like him."

"So, we're starting again?"

She was silent.

"Listen, Lori, I have nothing against him. We just met for ten seconds. Lighten up."

"At least he has ambition."

"Yeah?"

"Unlike you."

"Meaning?" I said.

"You went to college. The police thing was supposed to be temporary. You never launched. That put everything on my shoulders. I was depressed as a stockbroker. The coke helped to lift my mood so I could function at work. Then it took over. That's how I ended up sinking so low, with my lowlife boyfriend, Tom; how I ended up losing my trading license and standing here waiting to buy out the supply of porno vids with me on them."

"Maybe Lloyd will..."

I heard commotion in the house. April was at the front door. She seemed disheveled.

As Lori and I approached, I noticed April's earrings were off. She had one of the milk crates in her hands. "Let's get the hell out of here," she hissed.

"What about the DVDs?" Lori said.

April walked past me and motioned her head toward the car. She leaned back to balance the milk crate on her thigh. "Open the trunk."

As she stepped into the sun, I noticed a large red mark on her cheek. "What's going on?" I said.

"He's a fucking maniac is what's going on."

Lori took April's arm, shaking the contents of the crate. "What about the DVDs?"

"Lori, I just got smacked around for real up there. Forget the DVDs."

"I am not forgetting the DVDs," Lori replied. "That's why we came here."

"Let her go," I said.

"I want the fucking DVDs." Lori said.

"She says we should go," I said, "so we go. We'll deal with the DVDs later."

"No way."

"Lori," I said. "You think this isn't dangerous right now? You think we're not being watched from the house? Something went wrong. We need to get out of here and regroup. We can't ratchet this up while standing in his driveway with a virtual target on our backs. I want to get you two out of here, and then I'll come back for the DVDs, okay?"

"Fine," she said, walking past me to the car.

April dropped the crate on the gravel. "Trunk."

I opened the trunk and lifted the crate, putting it inside. The maid came out of the house. She was carrying the other crate and the garment bag. "This," she said.

"Thank you," April said, taking the crate from her and wedging it next to the other one. She closed the trunk with one hand and slung the garment bag over her back with the other. "That's it. Let's go."

We got in the car, and I drove a few blocks. April buried her head in her hands. Lori was in the back seat, staring out the window.

I pulled the car over and gently shook April's shoulder. "Are you okay with me leaving you here with Lori for a few minutes while I go back?"

"Just do what you've got to do," she said through her hair.

⚬⚬⚬

I walked back to the house and knocked on the front door. The maid answered. "Yes, again?"

I heard Len's voice from the living room. "Let him in, Aida."

I went inside. Len was seated on the couch, watching a baseball game on the flat-screen television. He had a slight paunch and gray hair at the temples. He wheezed when he breathed. "Lock Tourmaline."

"Len LeFontant."

"I was disappointed you left without saying good-bye. Lemonade?"

I perched on the edge of one of the wicker chairs. Its back cushion had the same blue fish motif as the cabana. "So, Len," I said, "what the fuck?"

"What?"

"Come on."

"It's nothing she's not used to."

Aida handed me a glass of lemonade. I put it on the coffee table. "She's used to play," I said, "not the real thing. Why did you kick the shit out of her?"

"Because, Lock, she brought poppers and such in her little bag of tricks. So, I kicked her out a little roughly. I won't tolerate that kind of thing in my home."

"That doesn't sound like her."

"So we have a 'he said, she said.'"

"You know what? Just give me the DVDs and the original master, and we'll put this unfortunate little adventure behind us."

"What DVDs?"

"My ex-wife, the girlfriends tape. You know what I'm talking about."

He smiled. "Yes I do."

"So?"

"Changed my mind."

"Really?"

"Only fair, the bitch reneged on the deal."

"Exactly how did she renege?"

"I didn't get blown. I get a headache if I don't get blown by a haughty bitch once a day."

"So, the plan was to get April down here so you could smack her around, but not do it in a dungeon owned by Cousin Bodacious because that would be disrespectful of your boss. And the DVD thing was utter nonsense just to make sure she showed up and blew you."

Len poured himself some more lemonade. "You know me too well."

"Well, that's not going to fly, Len."

He took a few gulps. "You hang out with that bitch a lot, don't you?"

"Her name is April."

"You ever notice how haughty she is, strutting her tits around at that dungeon, all the men falling all over themselves to kiss her high heels and grovel? I enjoy breaking those sorts of bitches." Something on the television caught his attention. The announcer was recounting a home run while it played in slow motion. "You have to admit she's not so haughty anymore."

"You know, you seem a bit haughty too, Len. Maybe once I get through with you, you won't seem so haughty anymore either."

He finished the rest of his lemonade. "Your job and mine, for that matter, is to keep the peace. Are you really going to break that peace over a whore who, by the way, works for Cousin Bodacious anyway?"

"She works in a dungeon that Bodacious has a silent interest in."

"Bullshit," he shouted. "That bitch works in a Cousin Bodacious operation, so she works for Cousin Bodacious. I'm the head of his security detail, so that means she also works for me. I can pay her, fuck her, or smack her around anytime I want. It's my call. And if she would have finished, instead of walking out like the whiney little bitch she is, I would have paid her, and I was also formulating the idea that if your ex-wife blew me, I might have given her back the DVDs. But that didn't happen, now did it?"

"Well, maybe when I leave you here lying in a pool of your own blood, you'll have time to consider how this day might have gone differently."

"We're done here," Len said, motioning to the stairs. There were two men standing there. One was tall and slightly stooped. He had on a blue blazer and tan slacks and had a full head of hair. The other was more filled out and shorter. He wore a white jacket and sunglasses. They walked toward me. The lanky one reached into his jacket for what appeared to be a holster.

I grabbed a porcelain vase and threw it at his face. He held up his hands to block it. That gave me about two seconds.

The mistake would have been to stand up. There was no time. I propelled myself out of the chair into a front roll, emerging to his left. As I came up, I hooked his leg and swept it. He fell forward, face down. I twisted around; knelt one knee into his back; and reached into his jacket, extracting his gun and stuffing it in my pocket.

He tried to push himself up. I circled my hands into a double palm heel strike to opposite sides of his neck. He curled into a ball, cradling his head in his hands.

The other kicked toward me. Still kneeling, I formed an X-block with my forearms, grabbing the ankle and locking onto it. He pulled his leg back, but I went with the movement, pushing him off balance. As he fell, I let go and shot a fingertip snake strike into his groin.

The first one got to his feet and lunged at me. I stood and straightened my arms, bringing the left down and the right up in a windmill crane technique. My wrists each made contact with his arm, locking it straight.

I immediately moved my arms the opposite way, reversing the windmill, scissoring his neck and back. He groaned but didn't fall. I terminated the movement with a hip toss. As he went down, I landed on top of him, pressing both hands into his upper abdomen, sealing his breath. He clutched his chest and stayed down.

The other grabbed me from behind. I shot an elbow into his groin. It was the second strike to that area, and this time, I used real force. He doubled up and also stayed that way.

Len clapped slowly. The sound echoed. He was leaning against the front door, holding a .38 revolver.

I crossed my arms. "Going to shoot me, Len?"

"Thought had crossed my mind."

"You understand that she is Grandfather's wife. Shooting me and beating her up is not the best survival strategy for you."

"You want to talk truth?" he said.

"Go for it."

"You know and I know that Susan Heung is vulnerable, the whole fucking family is. So far, we have coexisted more or less. Don't give me a reason to suggest to Cousin Bodacious that we change that."

"You couldn't just have had a session with her, Len? That wasn't enough? You had to beat her up for real?"

"Yes that's right, Lock. I had to beat her up for real."

"Well, fuck you."

"Fuck you too. Now that you got that out of your system, leave. And I don't want to hear any more from your cokehead ex-wife, either. The DVDs are spoken for."

"This is not over."

"Go."

CHAPTER EIGHT

I returned to the car. "Did you get the DVDs?" Lori said.

"I don't have them. If you want to go back there to discuss it with him yourself, be my guest, but I'm taking April home now."

"Asshole," she muttered.

❧

The day would not have been complete without being caught in summer shore traffic on the Parkway. Lori used the opportunity to share a few meaningful statements about her feelings on the day's events. Eventually, she lay along the back seat and closed her eyes.

April stared silently out the side window. There were two yellowish-bordered red splotches on her face. Every so often, she would rub her stomach and wince.

"Talk to me," I said softly, so as not to wake Lori.

"Nothing to say." The splotch on her right cheek prevented her mouth from fully opening. It reminded me of Grandfather's lopsided smile, though his was informed by a restrained wisdom and power. Hers was merely pained.

"No, tell me," I said.

"I don't want to talk about it." She maintained her gaze out the window. The traffic opened up after the Raritan toll plaza, and we began to move at a reasonable clip.

I stroked her back. There was a bump just under her shoulder. When I touched it, she winced and arched forward.

What would I tell Grandfather? I had been waiting around enjoying the beach while his wife and the mother of his child had been beaten like a stubborn mule. How could I face him?

Lori started to snore. After a while, I noticed April tearing up. She took my hand in both of hers and kissed it, a uniquely April thing to do. "Lock?" she mumbled into my hand.

"Yeah, kiddo?"

"I've been fighting it, but I really need to throw up."

I drove onto the shoulder and helped her out of the car. I half-carried her to some adjacent bushes, and held her abdomen, pressing in as she purged.

After she was done, I took a tissue from my back pocket and cleaned her mouth as best I could. I went back to the car and got a bottle of water from the back seat. I held it to her lips so she could gargle. She took the water into her mouth and spit it to the side.

"Ready?" I said.

She nodded. We began to walk back to the car and stopped.

"What?" I said.

She knelt on the grass. Her stomach started convulsing again. This time she did not produce anything.

I helped her stand. She gripped my forearm tightly. "I can't let him see me like this. Do you understand?"

"I think he would want to help you heal."

"No, listen to me," she said, digging her finger nails into my skin. "I can't."

"So, you want to camp out here on the Parkway?"

She laughed. "Yeah, let's set up a tent here for a year or two."

"Long as you want."

She shimmied herself onto the hood of the car. We watched the others whiz by. After a while, she said, "What I really want you to do is heal me, at least enough to make it look like I'm still in one piece. Not like this."

"I'm not as good at the Reiki as Grandfather." What an understatement.

"He says you're good—better than good."

"He's being charitable."

She rubbed the spot where she had imprinted my forearm with her fingernails. "You're all I've got right now."

"I'll try."

We reentered the car, and I drove to the next rest stop. The parked cars were mostly clustered by the McDonalds at the entrance. I pulled ours to the other side where the lot was empty.

Lori was still asleep. April maneuvered the back of her seat all the way down so the headrest was almost touching Lori's ankles. April lay back and closed her eyes.

Grandfather would routinely use Reiki treatments to help her with everything from her lumbosacral problems to menstrual cramps. It had become an accepted part of their marriage: he would immediately heal even her most minor discomfort. But this wasn't minor, and I wasn't him.

She was still wearing the tight, black minidress and translucent stockings. I slipped off her pumps and felt the bottoms of her feet. After a while I stopped. "I'm sorry," I said. "I'm not getting anything. Could you lose the pantyhose?"

She kept her eyes closed and reached under her dress, insinuating her thumbs into the waistband of the hosiery.

She arched herself and rolled them down her legs. When they were at her feet, she kicked them off.

"I'm going to need to touch you," I said.

"Just do whatever you need to do."

"No more words; just relax." I took her foot in my hand again. Grandfather's style of Reiki used the feet and palms, the gateways to the rest of the body, to diagnose. I pressed into the spot directly under her large toe, closed my eyes, and tried to connect.

I felt nothing. I lowered my fingers to her heel and kneaded it, using a reflexology technique to sense her energy. Still nothing.

"I'm not getting in," I said. "Show me the worst place."

She lifted the hem of her dress to just under her breasts. She was clean shaven, and there were thin, gold ring piercings on each labial lip. She took my hand and pressed it against her lower abdomen. "He punched me there, a bunch of times."

I ran my fingers over the area. Still nothing.

If only Grandfather were here.

I closed my eyes and breathed deeply.

The Buddhist Temple in Kauai, Hawaii; the red slats; the sun setting behind the curved cornices, each of which had a Japanese character carved into the tip, representing the four seasons; the stairs made of wood, brought to a high shine with an ancient concoction approximating varnish.

My deceased second wife, Janice, sitting on the first step, wearing a white dress, the one with the asymmetrical hem that was so flattering, hugging her knees to her chin, tilting her head and smiling at me.

"April, you need to help me with this," I said.

"How?"

"Take my hand. Bear down. Imagine you're gently rocking the energy free from the place that hurts; rock it into my fingertips in gentle waves. I'll pull while you push. But it has to be in waves. That's how energy like this flows."

"He says things like that too."

"Deep breaths."

I synchronized my breathing to April's. With each of her exhalations, I searched for the telltale tingling in my fingertips, circling my hand around her abdomen barely a half inch from the skin.

I began to sense her energy. There was a coarse unevenness to it. I moved my hands in small circles over the area.

My palms started to heat up.

Finally.

I lathed the energy up and down her body without making physical contact of any kind. I lightly pressed energy into the splotches, like moving small mounds of dry sand. When my palms reached her face, she started to cry.

Grandfather had taught me that when the Reiki was done properly, the patient would often burst into tears. A purging. "Let it out," I whispered. "Don't hold back."

I returned to her abdomen and centered on the largest welt. But the energy had hardened, like a scab. I tried to move it, but it would not dislodge.

She was crying more softly now. There was only one way to complete this. The way he had warned me about. Old school.

I took short, rapid breaths, absorbing the negative *chi* from the area of her welt. With each breath, I visualized myself metabolizing the energy of her injuries.

"That tingles," she whispered.

"Just relax."

Eventually, she stopped crying and fell into a deep sleep.

I did the same absorption technique to the splotches at her cheek. I took a five-minute break, turned her over, and did the same with the welt on her back.

Once I had done as much as I could, I pulled her dress down to her thighs and stuffed the pantyhose in her bag.

I watched her breathe. She was in a deep sleep. I checked on Lori. She was still sleeping, as well.

There was a heavy, leaden sensation in my groin. It filled and weighed me down. I got out of the car and fell onto the grass just over the curb.

I needed to expel this energy quickly. In a few hours, it would start to infiltrate my lymphatic system. I had to get rid of it now.

It was the first healing technique Grandfather had taught me when we had started the advanced internal training four years ago: the way to get rid of negative chi. It reminded me of when he had begun to teach me the basic Shaolin Kempo Karate system when I was a child. One of the first things we learned was how to fall without hurting ourselves. Getting rid of the negative *chi* was falling without hurting myself.

I took off my shoes and socks and stood in front of a large tree, placing my palms against the bark. I distantly heard the cars over the ridge on the Parkway.

I breathed slowly, drawing the *chi* from the Earth, the soil beneath me. I felt it travel through the soles of my feet, the inward gateway, up my legs, and through my spine. With another breath, I moved the tingling warmth through my arms and out my palms, the outward gateway, and into the tree. I moved the energy through my body in waves, just like Bette's uprooting push she had taught the kids at the karate school.

I maintained the rhythm, drawing the yin energy from the ground and expelling the yang energy through my palms.

Grandfather had originally explained it with the analogy of a garden hose. If there was dirty water caught in the hose, the best way to get rid of it would be to flush it out with the clean. I was flushing my body with clean *chi*.

When I was done, I sat with my back against the tree and fell asleep.

April tapped me. Her posture was relaxed and balanced again. The splotches on her face were still there, but the yellowing around the edges had dissipated. It seemed like several days of healing had taken place in the couple of hours since we had left Len.

She sat beside me, curling her smooth, bare legs beneath her dress and lying against the tree. "You're up," she said.

"Getting there."

"Thank you for all that."

"I wish I were better at it," I said.

"You did fine. You remind me so much of him sometimes. You have his feel."

"I'm nowhere near Grandfather's level. I wonder if I'll ever be."

"You're closer than you think."

"Maybe." I stood, brushing my pants. "You know, you were right that he is not long for this world."

"Thank you for finally saying that."

I looked up at the clouds. "With him leaving, I'm feeling pretty lost," I said.

"You're not lost. If you were, you never could have brought me back."

CHAPTER NINE

Lori refused to speak to either of us for the rest of the trip. We dropped her at her apartment in Hackensack. As I put the car in reverse to back out of her driveway, she hit my roof twice with her open palm. When I looked at her, she gave me the finger.

April lay down in the back seat. I glanced at her in the mirror from time to time. She had her hands over her eyes and seemed to be holding herself back from crying.

I called Pauline. She was going to know sooner or later. Just looking at April told most of the story. It was better Pauline heard it from me.

She listened quietly. About halfway through, she interrupted, "Stop in here before you drop her off."

"I don't know if that's such a good idea, Paulie."

"She works for me, and so do you for that matter. This is work-related. I want to see her."

"Fine."

We arrived at Pauline's house in Englewood Cliffs. She was on the phone and motioned us to sit on the couch in the living room. April lay down, and I covered her with one of the multicolored blankets Pauline had brought back from last year's trip to South America.

Pauline hung up the phone and brought April coffee on a sterling silver plate filled with cookies and European chocolates. "Have you called Grandfather?" she said.

"Not yet," I replied.

"You really don't want to call Grandfather?"

"Later," April said.

"Okay, tell me what happened," Pauline said.

April propped herself up. "At first, he was nice enough, kind of false gentlemanly. He called me 'young lady' and things like that. I took off my clothes, and he tied my wrists to the bed post.

"Then, his expression changes, and he yells at me in a mental sort of way. I'm still tied to the bedpost. And he climbs on top and *whap*." April smacked her fist into her open palm. "He punches me in the stomach a bunch of times. So I yell at him to stop, and he smacks me in the face a bunch more times, telling me to shut up and calling me names. So, I start to cry, and he says if I don't stop, he'll have people kill me, burn up my corpse, and throw me in a garbage dumpster so no one will find me.

"I can't push him away. I'm completely helpless. I continue to cry, and he finally stops and unties me, and I run downstairs. Then Lock got me the hell out of there."

"Anything else?" Pauline said.

"Only other thing I remember is that as I was getting dressed and gathering my equipment to leave the room, he was just sitting on the bed, ignoring me, staring at the floor, like some kind of zombie."

"Maybe he was high," Pauline said.

"No, it was like he was mental or something."

Pauline sat forward on the opposite couch. "Some random questions, sweetie?" she said.

April closed her eyes. "Sure, go ahead."

"Any penetration?"

"No."

"Sexual touching?"

"No."

"Drugs?" Pauline said.

"No."

"He said you were doing poppers," I said.

"No way."

"Did he pay you?" Pauline said.

"It was a freebie."

Pauline handed April a wad of cash with a rubber band around it. "There's two thousand dollars in that roll, for your trouble."

"But I did this behind your back. I violated your rules by freelancing."

"You made a mistake. You'll learn from it. You're going to lose some money while those bruises heal. This will tide you over."

"I don't deserve this," she said softly. "Not after what I did."

Pauline turned to me. "You dropped Lori off at her apartment?"

"Yeah."

"And you'll take April home?"

"Sure," I said.

"Come back after you do. We need to talk."

"Sounds ominous."

"It is."

❧

I drove to April and Grandfather's house. April applied makeup using the vanity mirror. The swelling on her face was darkening. "Look at me now," she said.

"You're still a very beautiful woman."

"I'm ugly."

"April, stop."

We arrived at their house.

"Oh, shit," April said. The monk named Franklyn was kneeling in front of the porch, chanting. There were two children standing next to their bicycles, watching from across the street. "Get that fucker away from my house, please."

I parked the car. Franklyn glanced at me as I walked toward him. I squatted. "Once again, I am in the difficult position of asking you to leave."

He ignored me and kept chanting.

"Please, this is neither the time nor the place."

He looked up at me and chanted louder.

I went back to the car. April lowered her window a crack. "Can you ignore him?" I said.

She closed her eyes. "No."

I went back to Franklyn and squatted on the grass again. He stopped chanting and stared at me. His eyes were a light, aquamarine blue. He was at least twenty years older than me, but his face was unlined. "You have been healing the mother," he said.

"How did you know that?"

"I can feel the Reiki."

"You can feel the Reiki?"

"Yes."

"Then you know that she needs peace and quiet to heal. Your presence is upsetting her."

"Why?"

"Because she knows you are here because Grandfather's leaving is imminent."

"It is. But please tell her we are not just here to chant for him. We are also here to chant for her and the child."

"Leave the child out of this, please. He's four years old."

"He won't be four years old forever."

"Can you just leave while I get her from the car to the house?"

He stood. "Of course."

❦

Grandfather was watching television with Fletcher. It was a program about little Japanese monsters fighting one another with Samurai swords.

"Mommy," Fletcher ran into April's arms. She bent on one knee and hugged him. He held her for a moment and then put his hand on her cheek. "This hurts."

"Yes," she said.

Grandfather joined us. He stared at her and looked at me. "You did work with her."

"As best I could." I glanced at Fletcher who was listening to our exchange.

Grandfather gingerly placed his fingertips on the crown of April's head. "I see." He gently lifted her chin so he could look into her eyes. "Are you all there, Plum Blossom?"

She nodded, not meeting his gaze. Fletcher hugged her leg. Grandfather stroked her hair, examining the discoloration on her face. "We can heal this more."

Fletcher rubbed April's lower abdomen through her short black dress. "Here too."

Grandfather knelt and put his hand over Fletcher's. "Yes, that's right."

She wiped her eyes. "I need to be alone for a while." She reached behind her for my hand. "Thanks again, Lock. We'll talk more later, okay?"

"Sure," I said.

She lifted Fletcher and went upstairs.

Grandfather called after her. "Apply sage and tiger balm."

I gripped Grandfather's shoulder. "I'm sorry. It should never have happened."

He opened the refrigerator and pulled out some orange juice. "What did happen?"

As I told Grandfather the story, I stared through the blinds at the front lawn. Franklyn was not there.

"Again, I'm sorry," I said.

He took some fruit from a tray. "Has she spoken to you about moving in here?"

"I think it's a bad idea."

"Why?"

"She's your wife."

"She would be a good woman for you. You would be a good father for our son."

"You would be a good father for your son."

He smiled.

"Don't you care enough about them to stay?" I said.

"If not for them, and you for that matter, I would have been gone a long time ago. You need to step in now."

"What if I can't?"

"You can, Little One." It was what he used to call me when I first started taking karate lessons from him as a small child. All those years ago.

I looked at my watch. "We can talk more later, but Pauline's waiting for me. I have to go."

❧

I drove to Pauline's home. As I pulled up, she approached the car and leaned on the passenger window. "Let's take a ride."

"Where to?" I said.

"The Binghamton. We need to talk, but I need a drink first."

The Binghamton was a ship docked in the Hudson River at a wharf in Cliffside Park. It had been converted into a high-end restaurant and lounge. Pauline and I often went there late at night to unwind after she came home from the dungeon.

She ordered red wine, and I had a Perrier with lime. We sat on two lounge chairs located at the stern. The Manhattan skyline was in full view.

She took a sip of wine and placed the glass on the white, wrought-iron table. The waitress gave us menus, but we left them face down. "I am angry at you," she said.

"I know."

"The way I run the dungeon, I meet these people and size them up and decide how much parental supervision is needed for them to play with my girls. None of that happened today, and this is the result."

I looked at her hands gripping the metal armrests. "You're right. I didn't exercise good judgment."

"And you deceived me."

"And I deceived you."

"So I'm going to have to fire you," she said.

"Paulie, isn't that an overreaction?"

"It's one thing to cheat on me."

"I never cheated on you."

"What I'm saying is that in a way, that would have been better than this. Here, you betrayed me financially. You undermined my management of my employees. You hurt me in a way you should not have."

"I understand."

"Come here." She took my hand.

"You going to toss me over?" I said.

"Just come here," she said, kissing me. It turned into a long embrace. I could hear two small motorboats a distance away. The sound of the engines receded.

She let go and held my lapel. "I am firing you."

"I heard."

"And not from my life, just from the dungeon."

"Firing me from your life is also coming soon," I said.

"Jesus," she said. "I so feel blue right now."

"You want me to drive you home?"

"Yeah, let's smoosh."

"After everything?"

She tugged on my shirt again. "Just for a little while. Just to know that part of us still works. Just a quick smoosh."

"I'm not in any mental state, Paulie. April got beat up because of me. Grandfather is dying. You're firing me."

"So, not tonight dear, I have a headache?"

I laughed. "Yeah, something like that."

She kissed me again. "The best reason of all to make love. In the face of all that, this. In the face of our impending end, this. A 'fuck you' to inevitability."

I shut my eyes. "But not just now, okay?" I said.

"Okay," she whispered.

CHAPTER TEN

Later that night, I arrived at Trudy Taylor's apartment building.
I followed the next person to buzz his way into the lobby.

I knocked on her apartment door. No one was there.
I went back to the lobby and waited.

Eventually, Jaegyu followed someone else through the
lobby's double doors and sat next to me. Jaegyu was wearing
a white, open-neck shirt and gray slacks with loafers.

"What are you doing here?" I said.

"You were supposed to bring me to your meeting with
the prison guard," he replied.

"So you followed me?" I said.

"This is where the prison guard lives."

"I know that."

"Ms. Heung asked you to bring me here, and you did
not."

"That's right."

About an hour later, Trudy Taylor came into the
building with two supermarket bags. "You again," she said.

I took the bags.

"Who's your friend?" she said.

"I work with Susan Heung," Jaegyu said, following us
into the elevator.

We entered her apartment. It was a studio. She had
painted the walls dark red. The furniture was black lacquer,
and there were wooden horse figurines in a lighted display
by the window.

I put the bags on the kitchen counter. Jaegyu stood in the corner. "Have you decided whether you'll help me get in?" I said.

"If I do," Trudy replied, "it needs to be reciprocal. Whatever you learn, you share with me. Nothing held back."

"Everything I learn, yes. But not my methods. Once I'm in there, I'm a free agent. You just get me in and get me out again."

She started to put the soup cans in one of the cabinets. "Can't agree to that," she said.

"Why not?"

"I need to know your source. I can't be in the position of letting you just gallivant around the prison to your heart's content. That's not developing a lead. That would just be irresponsible on my part."

"I can't tell you who my source is," I said.

"Then you're not getting in."

"He's meeting with Jason Heung's former cellmate, Roy Sokowsky," Jaegyu said. "He and Jason were homosexual lovers."

Taylor smiled at me. "There, that wasn't so hard, was it?"

I looked at Jaegyu. "Not at all."

Trudy closed the cabinet and wiped her hands with a dish towel. "Don't be upset," she said. "I already know all about Roy Sokowsky. In fact, I questioned him extensively. If you think you can get more information out of him, be my guest. Just don't hold back what you learn. If you do, your boss'll become my number-one suspect."

"He'll hold back nothing," Jaegyu said.

"Fine," I said. "The way we do this with the least hassle is that I'll be transferred as a detainee from the Fort Lee Municipal Jail to the prison temporarily. What would you need to do that?"

"A transfer form. Make it a material witness transfer to simplify things. They move material witnesses all the time from municipal jails." She looked at Jaegyu, who was staring at some papers on her coffee table. "Is your talkative friend going in too?"

"Just me."

She folded the rest of the bags and placed them in the cabinet under the sink. "Are we done?"

"Almost."

"What else?"

"Tell me about Bergenweld."

"Like what?"

"He's indirectly associated with the Bodacious people," I said. "What else?"

"That's all I know."

"And you?" I said.

"Am not."

"You're not?"

"You doubt that?"

"In other words, you work in that prison, and you have no relationship with Cousin Bodacious's people?"

"And that surprises you?"

"Just asking."

"Why, because I'm black like Cousin Bodacious?"

"No, because you work in a prison that Cousin Bodacious essentially owns."

"I think it's because I'm black. Let me tell you something. We come in many types. There's the sadist misogynist pigs like Cousin Bodacious and Len LeFontant, and then there's people like me just doing their job and counting down the years to their pensions. Cousin Bodacious doesn't own me. No one owns me—not you and not him."

"Fair enough."

"And to answer the question you posed last time, I do know that if my investigative report implicates Cousin Bodacious, it will go from Lt. Bergenweld to the shredder in one simple toss, but that doesn't mean that I'll do anything differently. It means that I will do the right thing, and someone else will do the wrong thing. And by the way, you never know. Lt. Bergenweld might not shred it. There's a lot of levels here."

"When does your shift start tomorrow?"

"Three in the afternoon."

"By one, I'll be detained by the Fort Lee police. You'll need to go there and take custody of me. Once we're at Rahway, I'll need to see Jason's cellmate as quickly as possible. Then you can transport me back before your shift is over."

"East Jersey."

"What?"

"The name of the prison. Stop calling it Rahway. People will make you as an old cop."

"The important thing is that once we're in, you'll get me to Sokowsky. I was going to do it without you, but since my better half here disclosed to you who I'm meeting with, I figure you can get me there faster."

"If the paperwork from Fort Lee says you're a material witness."

"The paperwork from Fort Lee will say that. Will it be enough to suspend your normal duties?"

"It should," she said, "and I want to be clear. When I get you out, you tell me everything you learned."

"He will learn nothing of importance," Jaegyu said.

"I think it's time for you and your weird friend to leave," she said.

❧

Jaegyu and I walked down the stairs to the lobby and out the back exit. I could see the bay a few blocks away down the hill. There were two motorboats racing along the coast, leaving white foam in their wake.

"Why did you tell her our source?" I said.

"She already knew," Jaegyu replied.

"We couldn't be sure of that."

"She knew."

"Wouldn't it make more sense for you to do your own investigation while I do mine, and then we compare notes?"

"I am performing my own investigation," he said. "And we will not compare notes."

"Fine."

"The prison guard is playing you for a fool," he said.

"Really?"

"Yes."

"How so?"

"She is lying to you."

"I assumed she was not telling me everything. You think she's working for Bodacious?"

"I did not say she is working for Bodacious."

"So, you're basically saying that there are unanswered questions. That's exactly why I need to get into the prison to see what I see."

"You will see nothing," he said.

"So, what do you suggest, genius?"

"That you return to your karate school and focus on organizing birthday parties for six-year-olds. I will handle this investigation."

"A foreigner who has no ties to law enforcement will handle a murder investigation in New Jersey better than a former New Jersey detective?"

"Yes," he said.

"I have a different suggestion. Why don't you go fuck yourself?"

❧

The next day, I went to the Fort Lee Police Station. The borough had just added green flags to each of the antique-style street lights along Main Street. They read, "Fort Lee. Leading New Jersey's Renaissance." The one near the post office a block from the police station had come loose and was dangling as it whipped in the wind.

I had to wait for Lt. Attia to return from inspecting a crime scene. Lorraine Chrysocolla told me some teenage boys had been throwing lit firecrackers across Route 9W. One had exploded on a woman's windshield.

Sam nodded to me as he came through the waiting area. He was wearing a blue windbreaker with the words *Strike Force Commanding Officer* stenciled on the back. In addition to his other duties, he was the head of the Bergen County Organized Crime Strike Force. It was the coordinating body for the local police efforts of all the municipalities in Bergen County conducting operations against organized crime.

I followed him into the basement cafeteria. "Kids are assholes," he said. "Coffee?"

"Yeah. Injuries?"

"The woman had a concussion. Maybe it will teach her that the best response to being surprised while driving is not to steer across the highway and smash into a tree."

"How is this something you are handling?"

"I'm covering for someone. What's the difference?"

"Polite conversation."

"Why are you here?" He ran the tap water before washing his hands.

I closed the door, locking it from the inside, and explained the plan to him.

"It's a bad idea," he said.

"I have no other choice. I need to get information, and it is all inside that place. That's where I need to be."

"I find it very interesting that Susan Heung isn't going into the prison herself. She'll be sitting in her Jacuzzi at the Palisadium while you get a shiv in the back."

"What's the alternative?" I said. "Jason Heung gets murdered and nobody cares?"

"Nobody does care," he said. "Get it through your head. I know I don't care. You're risking your life for nothing."

"My life to risk."

"Why should I cooperate?" he said.

"So don't. I'll just commit a crime and you'll have to lock me up anyway."

"With the budget cuts in this town, you could steal the chief's car, and we'd just take down a report for the insurance company."

"Sam, just do this, okay?"

He took off his windbreaker and folded it over his arm. "All right, fine."

"Thank you ... Jesus."

He smoothed his hand over his scalp. "So, you trust this guy who's bringing you down there?"

"It's a she, and I trust her to a point."

"Anything you learn, you share with me. Anything."

"I thought the brother's murder was out of your jurisdiction."

"So what?"

"Thanks."

"You're welcome." He shouted into the hallway, "Lorraine?"

"He giving you trouble?" Lorraine said. She was wearing an expanded blue police shirt that barely fit over her abdomen.

"Put through the paperwork to have this one detained as a material witness. One of the guards from East Jersey Prison will pick him up later for transport."

Lorraine smiled. "Finally, justice is done." She took a pair of handcuffs from her belt holder. "Assume the position, slimeball."

"Lorraine, I thought you only used handcuffs on your girlfriends."

"The fur-lined ones. The uncomfortable steel ones I save for you."

CHAPTER ELEVEN

Later that night, I sat in a cell at the East Jersey Prison. Taylor had transported me from the Fort Lee Jail as planned. After all that trouble, the administrator at the prison barely looked at the paperwork.

She parked me in a solitary cell at a holding area for men awaiting trial. That way, she could easily bring me out again after my meeting with Jason's cellmate.

It took her three hours to find and move him to my area of the prison. Taylor placed him in my holding cell and locked us in. "Twenty minutes," she said.

The fact that Sokowsky had become Jason's lover cut both ways. I had no way of knowing if Sokowsky was informing to Cousin Bodacious or was his sworn enemy. It was part of the reason I wanted this meeting to be in person.

He was my height, with a blond crew cut and thin, angular facial features. He sat on the cot and stared at me. "Who are you?" he said.

"I work for Susan Heung."

"And?"

"I have some questions."

"Such as?"

"Who killed Jason Heung?"

"I don't know."

"Were you part of it?"

"No."

"Did he have any friends here, anyone he would have confided in?"

"No one. And he didn't confide in me."

"Enemies?"

"Everyone. You want all his stuff to give back to his sister?"

"Sure."

Sokowsky reached in his pocket and pulled out a round piece of jewelry. "Nose ring."

I took it. "They let you guys wear jewelry in here?"

"Some of us."

"Has anyone else spoken to you about Jason since the murder?"

"The girl guard and a Japanese guy."

"Could he have been Korean?"

"Sure, why not?"

"Describe him."

"Wears a suit."

"Gray suit?"

"Yeah."

"What did he say?"

"Wanted to know about his daily routine, who were his friends on the inside, his meetings with that lieutenant about cooperation."

"Lt. Attia?"

"Yeah."

"What did you tell him?"

"Nothing to tell. I don't know anything."

"What else?"

"He also said that another guy might come by asking questions."

"Like I am."

"He said I should keep my mouth shut."

"How much did he give you?"

"A thousand in small bills."

"You want more?"

"Jason promised that the Heungs would give me a job when I get out in a couple of months. What I want is confirmation that it's going to happen."

"I'll look into it. You know anything at all that can help me find out who did this?"

"All I know is I didn't kill him."

"Were there threats against him?"

"All the time. This prison is ninety percent dark. Asians are not welcome."

"You're white. How is it for you?"

"Just fine. What about the job?"

"If you don't help me, there's not going to be a job."

"It was promised."

"So far, you've given me nothing."

"Then I'm not saying another word."

"You change your mind, you tell that guard that brought me in to get a hold of me."

"The girl?"

"Right.

Taylor countersigned release papers for me to be remanded back to the Fort Lee Municipal Jail. She handcuffed me, and we went to her car. As we drove off, she gave me the key to unlock them. "What did he say?" she asked.

"Answer a question for me first. You ever see that guy before, the one that was with me when I met you at your apartment yesterday?"

"The weird guy?"

"Right, the weird guy. You ever see him before?"

"No."

"If he approaches you without me present, can you tell me?"

"I'll see if I can fit it into my busy schedule. Now what did Sokowsky say?"

I told her.

"So, he was less than helpful."

"Essentially," I said.

"You know it is possible that Cousin Bodacious had nothing to do with this."

"Possible," I said.

"Perhaps your boss?"

I closed my eyes and leaned back in the seat. I was so tired, I could have fallen asleep then and there. "I don't know. I have some ideas, but again, who knows?"

She rubbed her hand along the steering wheel. "I know what you're thinking."

"What?"

"You think it might have been that weird guy, the Korean."

"Thought had crossed my mind," I said.

"So Jason pissed off his own people and they killed him."

"I don't know enough to say that. I have a meeting scheduled with Susan Heung tomorrow. I'll have some questions for her."

"So she's paying you to investigate her brother's murder, and you end up investigating whether her people murdered him?"

"Among other suspects."

"You want some advice?"

"No."

"You should walk away from this one," she said. "It's dirty all around."

"Can't do that."

"Why not?"

"Promises to keep."

"What does that mean?"

I closed my eyes. "It means I have miles to go before I sleep."

When we arrived in Fort Lee, she signed me over to the jail administrator. He logged me in and placed me in a cell. About a half hour later, Lt. Attia called from home to have them release me.

∽

The next day, I met Susan Heung for lunch at a Korean restaurant on Route 9W near the nature preserve. It was on the bottom floor of a free-standing, red brick building. We sat at a table in the corner. Two decorative screens had been arranged as a courtesy to shield her from view. Susan ordered grilled tofu with red spices. I had the barbecue chicken.

"Brief me on your meeting in the prison," she said.

I did.

"What is your next move?"

"Not sure. Can I promise him a job?"

"We can find him something."

"Good."

She stared at the large, round table in the center of the restaurant. "That's where my father was murdered."

"I was here."

"As I recall," she said, "you physically carried me out of this place when the shooting started."

"And you lived to tell the tale."

She smoothed her hand along the surface of the wooden table. It made a soft brushing sound. "I'm going to insist that you cooperate more with Jaegyu."

"While he's filling your ear with more nonsense about me?"

"Is it all nonsense?"

"He's got divided loyalties," I said. "I don't. I would never betray you. He would in a second."

"Even more of a reason for the two of you to work together. You can have the benefit of his involvement, but also keep an eye on him."

"That's not enough of a reason."

"He has resources we do not have."

"Like what?"

"The Korean government."

"How does that help you? This is a local New Jersey prison killing, not nuclear disarmament. His contacts are not helpful here. He's just messing things up. Were you aware that he met with Jason's cellmate at the prison before I did?"

"No."

"Neither was I. He's not sharing what he learns with me, but I'm supposed to share everything with him. What do we know about his background?"

"Before BOK, he used to be affiliated with the South Korean government. He still has contacts there."

"How did you fall into bed with these guys in the first place?"

"I told you. They are financing us."

"No, I mean originally."

"Decades ago, my father developed high-level contacts in Seoul, both banking and governmental interests. He needed all the help he could get when dealing with Newark.

In those days, it was the Italians, not Cousin Bodacious. That came much later. We have never been more than a third of Newark in terms of manpower, political contacts, funding. My father needed to equalize the situation."

"Can't you just get Jaegyu to back off for a week or two?"

"I told you they have offered to involve themselves in avenging my brother's murder. It would be insulting to refuse."

"Name one thing he can do that I can't."

"He has favors he can call in with the US government, the FBI, NSA, etc."

"The National Security Agency is going to help us take on Cousin Bodacious?"

"Who knows? Maybe."

"Jesus."

"Just work with him."

"Fine."

"And keep me apprised."

❧

It was cloudy that afternoon. I rolled down my car window and drove along the Palisades. The air was cool. I reached a long stretch of Route 9W with no other vehicles on it. I accelerated to eighty miles per hour and put the car in neutral.

It felt like floating. There was no sound, except the whistling of air passing through the car. I breathed deeply. This would be a fine way to go. Just veer off over the guardrail into the Hudson River. A variation of what Grandfather was doing.

My cell phone vibrated. It was Cho. "What's going on?" I said.

"The DNA test you had us order from that lab you gave us came back on a preliminary finding. It was Jason."

"Well, that's something."

"And just to be double sure, I wanted to take another sample. I had someone call down to the prison, and guess what? The body has been misplaced."

"Jesus."

"They're looking for it and will get back to us when they find it."

"Could this get anymore fucked up, Cho?"

"Actually, there is more. You free to talk?"

"Sure.

"You know where my campaign office is on Fort Lee Road?"

"Yeah, yeah, I've only been there fifty times for bodyguarding."

"Lock, even I haven't been there fifty times."

"The point is I know it," I said. "And no Jaegyu, by the way."

"No Jaegyu."

CHAPTER TWELVE

Cho's office was a storefront a few blocks down the hill from the Fort Lee Municipal Building. It had a large outer area with a dozen desks and a walled-off conference room in the back. The last time I had been there I had provided security for Susan and him the night he lost the congressional election. At the time, the place had been packed with dozens of people who slowly exited as it became clear Cho was going to lose. He had kept the space and was actively preparing for another try.

The front door was open, and I locked it behind me. The outer room was dark, except for a small sliver of light that emanated from under the closed conference room door. I knocked and opened it.

Cho was at the head of the table, reading from a small pile of papers. There was a glass of red wine next to him. He motioned me to sit and slid a letter in my direction. It was a telecopy from the prison. "Lo and behold, no body," he said. "We're checking into it and will get back to you. Have a nice day."

"Not good," I said. "But the DNA was a match."

"Perfect match."

"So, the body missing doesn't change the fact that we know it was Jason."

"Yeah, but still."

"I know."

"Where are you in your investigation so far?" he said.

"I questioned Jason's cellmate and didn't find much, except that he had already spoken to Jaegyu, which I found strange. Oh yeah," I said, taking the nose ring out of my pocket and handing it to Cho, "something to remember your almost-brother-in-law by."

Cho held it up to the light and put it in his pocket. "The cellmate gave this to you?"

"Yeah."

"Can we get any more information from him?"

"The answer is I think so. He wants the job Jason promised before he was killed. I spoke to Susan, and she's fine with it. I'll be going back in to speak with him again to relay that. I expect he'll give me more information once I do."

"Let me know what happens with that," he said.

"Along those lines, there's something I wanted to ask you. For the last year, you were working directly with Susan on arranging for a reduced sentence in return for Jason testifying for the State concerning Bodacious. I was kept out of that. All I know is that there was a proffer to Attia about Bodacious, and I know it went nowhere. Tell me the rest."

"It's what you just said."

"Tell me more," I said.

"There's not much to tell. Susan had me approach Attia to get him out of there and put in witness protection in return for a proffer about Bodacious."

"With Jason's knowledge?"

"We got word to him through the cellmate's lawyer that there was a deal being discussed, but not the specifics. Attia debriefed Jason about three times, and the word that came back to me—"

"From?" I asked.

"An intermediary."

"The lawyer?"

"Lorraine Chrysocolla. The word came back from her that Jason really could not provide significant direct evidence about Bodacious, which made sense, since they were rivals. Besides, everything Jason would know would be secondhand hearsay. Not admissible as evidence."

"And that was it?" I said.

"Until we learned last week that Jason had been murdered. And I called you."

"And we assumed it was Bodacious."

"And Susan suspects Attia had some role in it," he said.

"Yeah, Attia kills a prisoner who fails to give him sufficient evidence against a drug lord. That has the ring of truth to it."

"She's not seeing this rationally," he said.

"Right, the rational assumption is that Jason did know something about Bodacious that he could use to bargain for his release, and that became known at the prison. Bodacious found out and then killed him. Bodacious owns that place. He could torture Jason for days to find out what he told Attia."

"But there's a missing piece to all that," he said. "If Attia was getting information from Jason about Bodacious, why didn't Attia have him moved? Why didn't he anticipate that Jason would be a target?"

"That's Susan's point."

"And it's a good one," he said. "Why keep him there?"

"Susan thinks Attia wanted him left there so he could be killed," I said.

"But why?"

"I don't know."

"Dead end," he said.

"So, let's talk about Jaegyu," I said. "He was at the prison questioning the cellmate. He fits the description that the cellmate gave me of a man who met with him."

"Right, because Jaegyu is conducting his own investigation."

"He has an agenda, Cho."

"No doubt."

"And that agenda may not be Susan's agenda. What do you know about him?"

"Not much," he said. "I don't involve myself with her South Korean contacts."

"What if Jaegyu murdered Jason? If the people Jaegyu represents found out that Jason was informing to law enforcement, they might not have made the subtle distinction between his informing about Bodacious and informing about them, or at least potentially informing about them."

"But how would Jaegyu arrange a murder in a prison owned by Bodacious?" he said.

"I got in there undercover without much trouble. All you need is someone with boots on the ground, like Trudy Taylor. There are probably another two dozen Trudy Taylors willing to get someone in there for a price—probably a rather small price."

"And to throw us off, we know who Jaegyu is accusing," he said.

"Me."

"You," he said.

"Which makes sense, since that way he undermines the credibility of any evidence I might find against him. It also causes Susan to be suspicious of me, which further strengthens his relationship with her."

"He talks about you all the time. Doesn't say very nice things."

"Such as that I would be involved in covering up Jason's murder?"

"Yes."

"On what basis?"

"First, you work as a bodyguard for the sex club in North Bergen."

"It is not a sex club. It's a BDSM dungeon. There's no sex allowed."

"You want to talk about that or this?"

"That," I said.

"Let's talk about this. The dungeon is owned by Cousin Bodacious. Your girlfriend works for him."

"But my relationship with Pauline has been rocky recently. We're having issues. Doesn't Jaegyu take that into account?"

"Your girlfriend owns a dungeon in which Bodacious is a silent partner. She sends him money every month, employs you as a bouncer, and shares your bed."

"When you say it like that, it does sound suspicious."

"And your asshole buddy is Len LeFontant, Bodacious's head of security."

"Susan encouraged me to befriend Len so we would have a means of resolving minor disputes between the Heung and Bodacious operations. Anyway, right now he's not my biggest fan."

"And all this brings up me," Cho said.

"You?"

"If she decides that you are a liability, it is not a big leap to decide I'm a liability too. I introduced you to her. I got you the bodyguarding gig. In her mind, you and I are completely linked. Your screw-up is my screw-up. Your betrayal is my betrayal."

"So Attia is blamed for Jason's death, and I am blamed for Attia's involvement, and you are blamed for introducing me to Susan, and this is the woman you're marrying in a couple of days?"

"Married. We eloped on our last trip to Seoul. This week is just going to be the reception."

"Why did you elope?"

"She wanted to be married under Korean law. Remember I said on the phone there were some other things I needed to tell you? She's moving the entire family operation to Korea in just a few weeks. She has a compound there ready to go. She's already hired people, set up an office, and so forth."

"An office for what?" I said.

"Export to the US."

"She's moving everything?"

"You know how she refers to the fact that Jaegyu's people are going to refinance the New Jersey real estate, the office parks and such?"

"Yeah."

"That's not exactly accurate. The way it is really going down is that they are financing a buyout. That's what she means by refinancing. It's really just financing to cash her out of everything."

"Everything—meaning the real estate and the stuff that's not on the up and up, as well?"

"Everything."

"So, Jaegyu is her ticket out."

"Which is why Susan can refuse him nothing. If he wants to investigate Jason's murder, if he wants you outright fired, he gets it. Jaegyu is running the table."

"So what do I do, Cho?"

"Find out what actually happened to Jason quickly. Do it now, because you don't have much time."

"Couldn't agree more." I started toward the door.

"And one more thing. Be careful of that woman prison guard."

"Trudy Taylor?"

"Just watch your step with her."

"Why?" I said.

"Jaegyu was also ranting and raving about her. He thinks she's aligned with Bodacious."

"There's no evidence of that."

"Jaegyu says he has evidence."

"Do me a favor. Tell Jaegyu to shut the fuck up for a change."

"Next time I see him, I'll mention it."

"Good," I said.

"Or maybe not."

✿

Late that afternoon, I drove to the karate school. The light was on. Bette was practicing her Tai Chi sword form. I watched her, propping my foot on one of the white plastic chairs on which the parents usually sat.

The red threaded sash twirled around the handle. She jumped-kicked at an imaginary opponent, coming down into a crouch with one leg extended to sweep the attacker to the ground. She followed with a front roll and twirled the sword in a blur of figure eights.

Bette was Janice's biological child. The last promise I had made to Janice before she died was to adopt Bette. Even though she was sixteen years old by then, I had done so.

She finished the form and put the sword back on the wall. "How did I do?" she said.

"It was solid, needs a little work here and there, but quite solid."

"April is upstairs."

"She's here now?" I said.

"Yeah, upstairs, why does she look like that, her face all beat up? What happened to her?"

"Long story."

"You need me to stay?"

"For my safety?"

"She does seem pretty needy."

I started to walk up the stairs. "Continue your Tai Chi sword form."

"Watch yourself," she called after me.

"I have 911 on speed-dial."

April was sitting on my bed in jeans and an oversized plaid shirt I recognized as Grandfather's. The bruising on her face had turned dark purple. Her lip was swollen.

I closed the door behind me. "What's going on?" I said.

"I just spoke to Lori. She is not a happy camper. She still wants me to help her get the DVDs."

I sat next to April. The bed sagged. "What does she want you to do, go back to Len and get beat up a second time?"

"Be nice. She's fragile."

"And you came over to tell me this?"

"That and to tell you my body aches. Can you give me another treatment?" She reached in her bag and pulled out Grandfather's cedar dragon box of acupuncture needles.

"I thought Grandfather was going to treat you from now on."

"I like the way you do it."

"Okay, lie down."

She lay on the bed and closed her eyes. I placed needles in the side of her jaw and the underside of her wrist. I rolled them softly between my fingers until I felt the energy feedback. "How does that feel?"

"Tingles," she said.

"Give it about ten minutes."

I inserted an instrumental CD into my boom box. It played a soft Chinese song performed with a single reed instrument. I took off my shoes, lowered the lights, and lit some incense.

After a while, she said, "Lock." Her eyes were still closed.

"Yeah?"

"What do I do when he dies?"

"There are a lot of people who will take care of you and Fletcher."

"I'm not so sure," she said.

"Count on it."

"Take the needles out."

"We're not done."

"Please."

I dislodged the acupuncture needles and put them in an empty cup.

When I turned again, she had sat up and taken off her shirt. Her breasts were small and punctuated with hard, brown nipples.

"What's this about?"

"You know what this is about," she said.

"I'm still with Pauline. Why do this to someone who trusts you?"

"She hates me."

"She just gave you two thousand dollars to tide you over after you did outcall against her wishes. This is how you repay her?"

"She did that to make a point."

"To me?" I said.

"No, to me."

"What are you talking about?"

"Men are so dense sometimes."

"What point?" I said.

"That she has two thousand dollars to support me and you do not. It was meant to undermine your manhood in my eyes."

"Did it work?"

"No."

"This is getting way too involved."

"She assumed what is going on, or is about to."

"April."

"Anyway, Pauline would never need to know for certain."

"Yeah, right, that's exactly how things work. People cheat and no one finds out for certain. That's the way it goes every single time."

She reached under my shirt and stroked my abdomen. "Don't be so tense."

"April, come on."

"Hush," she said. She took my hand and placed it on her left breast.

"You should leave," I said.

"You say as you continue to massage my nipple."

The reed music reached the end. After a moment, it started from the beginning again. I moved to the underside of her breast. *So soft.* "April, come on."

"Oh, forget it," she said, crouching on the floor and covering her face with both hands.

I tried to lift her by the shoulders.

"No, get off," she said, pushing me away.

"Come on, April."

"Can't you just make me feel like a desirable woman again?" she said through her hands. "Is that asking so much?"

"What are you talking about?"

"He beat me, Lock. He beat me, and then he spit on me for good measure."

"Wait, he spit on you?"

"For good measure. In my face."

"You know, I really should just go down there and kick the shit out of him."

"Forget him. That's not why I told you." She stood and embraced me with both arms.

"Fuck it. You win," I said, lifting her onto the bed and unsnapping her pants. I rolled them down her legs and over her feet.

She giggled. "So damn easy."

"Look who's talking."

❧

We made love for a long while. Afterward, I caressed her back lightly. She placed her hand on my chest, twirling her finger in small circles. "I'm leaving Grandfather," she said. "I'm taking Fletcher and going."

"Grandfather needs you now."

"He does not need me. He has made that abundantly clear."

"I disagree."

"It's not your decision to make."

"You still shouldn't do it."

"First thing I'm going to do tomorrow is move my stuff to the guest bedroom. Then, over the next few weeks, if he lasts that long, I'm going to look for an apartment. If not, I'll just sleep in the guest bedroom until he does his thing. Either way, you should move in with me."

"Is that what today was about?"

"Kind of."

"To give me a preview of things to come?"

"I know you'll be a good father to Fletcher. I can be good for you too, maybe bring you a little bit out of that darkness you're always in. Help you fill your life back up again with a living woman, rather than the memory of one who has passed."

"April, I can't—"

She cut me off with a kiss, rolling on top. "Round two."

❧

I put on a robe and went downstairs while April flipped through my music CDs for something "happier."

The lights in the karate studio were out. Bette had left. I gathered a half-empty bottle of wine from the refrigerator and a couple of glasses. I sliced some gouda cheese and soda crackers on a cutting board and brought the entire arrangement upstairs.

She met me at the door, taking the tray. She set it on my bureau and poured two glasses of wine. She placed a slice of cheese on one of the crackers, handing it to me.

"Always the hostess," I said.

"My feminine nature."

"What now?"

"You tell me," she replied. We held up our glasses in a toast and drank.

"Here's what I think," I said. "Nothing changes at all. We don't avoid one another, but we don't seek this out again. If it happens, it happens."

"That's so you."

"We don't ignore it. We just let things unfold."

"So passive," she said.

"We each have people counting on us. It's a moving train. We can't just step off. We've got to wait for the next stop."

She ate a slice of cheese. "You mean Grandfather's death."

"Yes, primarily, and the effect it is going to have on everyone around us, from Fletcher to Pauline to Bette to the two of us. As I said, we let it unfold."

"That doesn't work on my timetable," she said.

"Why not?"

"Because I'm totally and completely in love with you, Mr. Lock Tourmaline. More tonight than ever."

I was silent.

She nudged me. "Don't you have something you want to say to me?"

"Like?"

"Like that you love me."

"Yeah, I guess I do."

She laughed. "Don't get all emotional on me now."

"Sorry. I'll dial it back."

CHAPTER THIRTEEN

I napped for about a half hour and was woken by my cell phone.

April was gone. There was a note taped to the lampshade by the bed. *Got to relieve the babysitter of the munchkin. PS—Don't forget. You can't deny it anymore.*

I looked at the Caller ID. It was Len LeFontant. I put the phone to my ear. "Yes, Len," I said.

"I have your nut case here again," he said. "She came into my house and pulled a gun on me."

"No."

"You should also know that she tripped the burglar alarm and the Elberon Police came."

"They going to charge her?"

"I interceded, out of respect."

"Where is she now?"

"Still here. You need to come down and get her."

❧

When I arrived at the Elberon house, Len was waiting outside, sitting on the stoop by the cabana. It was getting dark. The white halogen security lights cast harsh shadows along the gravel driveway.

He motioned me to sit next to him. The top joint of his right pinky finger was gone. It had been severed a few years ago in what he had described as some sort of boating accident. I had other thoughts on how that particular injury had occurred, such as perhaps Cousin Bodacious doing a Yakuza on him to set an example when things did not go well. "Where is she?" I said.

"Just sit for a moment."

"Why?"

"Organized crime summit."

"Stop the bullshit. I want to see her."

"You do understand that we bought the rights to that video from the creep who shot the film of her. It's legally ours. In fact, the only illegal thing is that she broke into a private home and threatened the inhabitant with a gun, which in this case, as crazy as it sounds, happens to be me."

"Len, why are we out here and not in there?"

"You have to understand that she has now been down here twice trying to get me to give up Cousin Bodacious's property, the latest time with a gun."

"Yeah, yeah, and?"

"We smacked her in the face a few times. I won't lie to you and say we were wrestling the gun away from her. That took about three seconds. We bitch-slapped her a few times afterward to make the point. Nothing major, nothing she hasn't experienced before, given her nature, but I'll be honest, fairly hard, and again, just to make the point. I expect she'll whine to you about that. So, I wanted you to hear it from me first, in case you have any questions. I am admitting to you she was bitch-slapped."

"Got it. No big deal; just a few well-deserved bitch-slaps."

"What did you expect, that I would throw her a beach party?"

"Perfectly reasonable to beat up two women in two days. Very manly on your part. I'm sure you're the proudest man in Elberon right now."

"I bitch-slapped her. I did not beat her up. There's a big difference."

"So, I should thank you for only bitch-slapping her?"

"Listen to me," he said, raising his voice. "I am the victim here."

"Really?"

"She broke into my house and pulled a gun on me. Nobody gets away with that. Nobody. She is lucky it wasn't a bullet to the head. I held back and made it just a few slaps out of respect for you."

"Len, why can't you just give her the fucking DVDs? Is it really worth all this drama? Is Bodacious running out of pornography?"

"You know, it's bigger than that, Lock. Half this game is perception. If it gets around that Cousin Bodacious gave in to a civilian, even in this small way, you know what will happen. There will be people challenging us in bigger ways, and they won't be sexually frustrated suburban bitches. They'll be Russians with Glocks. They'll be the crazy South Koreans you associate with, or maybe the old Italians catching their second wind, ready to take back Newark from the Mullies. This cannot go on. I will not allow it."

"What does that mean?"

"It means that the next time, my people will put a bullet in her head and dump her somewhere."

"If that ever happened, you'd be the next one dumped somewhere with a bullet in your head."

He looked up at the night sky. "Okay, how about this? Next time it happens, I will release to our contacts in the local media enough information about congressional candidate Henry Cho that he will never run for anything again. We'll use our people in the State Attorney General's Office to see to it that it becomes publically known that

his wife financed his campaign with money from the family
real-estate venture, which is kept liquid with proceeds
from the drug distribution business. The money he used
in the campaign was fruit of the poisonous tree, and that's
conspiracy to money launder. And when the dust clears, I
will visit the newlyweds in their respective prison cells and
let them know that this all happened because you were not
man enough to control your loopy ex-wife."

"Prick."

"That's me, the big, black prick. And you're blameless,
right? What is it you always say? You work for criminals,
but you are not one of them? Horseshit. Total horseshit."

"When you say it like that, it does seem kind of flimsy."

"I'm not kidding around, Lock. I respect you, and I
particularly respect your skills. You have the best hands
I've ever seen, and I've seen many. But I am telling you
to back off. If you do something here you shouldn't, and
you ignite something that shouldn't be ignited, which the
Heungs are not prepared for to say the least, you will have
brought down the entire Heung operation that you are
hired to protect, and it will be for nothing, for some nutty
suburban bitch who brought this on herself by letting her
boyfriend tape her doing the one thing she does well. So
who will really be the prick here?"

I stood, brushing the dirt off my pants. "This is getting
old. Just let me take her and get out of here."

"Right, take her home, tuck her in, and thank God she
is your ex-wife, emphasis on ex."

We went inside. In addition to the two bodyguards
from the last time, there were now three others. They
were in the living room watching a sports interview on the
widescreen television.

"You added a few new faces."

"Yes I did."

"With me in mind?"

"Don't flatter yourself."

"So, you just happened to invite more members of the mouth breathers association to watch the game with you?"

"All right, it was with you in mind."

"Where is she?" I said.

"Bathroom," one of the men replied. He nodded at me. He was one of the two I had fought.

"Tell her I'm here, please."

Len handed me a beer from the coffee table. "Want one?"

"No thanks," I said, putting it down on the granite kitchen table top.

"Want to watch television for a while?"

"Len, isn't there anything we can offer you to get back those DVDs? If I can get more money, maybe triple cost? Come on, there has to be something."

"We're done discussing it," he said, taking a long sip of his beer.

A commercial for shaving cream came on the television. "Also, while we have this moment to share, I was thinking you might ask Cousin Bodacious if he wants to confess to Jason Heung's murder. You know, just out of respect."

"Cousin Bodacious did not kill Jason Heung. Of that, I am certain."

"How can you be certain?"

"Because any such move might well result in a war, and we have contingency plans for beefing up security for Cousin Bodacious dramatically in preparation for a war, as I am sure you do for Susan Heung. He would never take that kind of step without including me, and I was not included."

"So then who killed him?"

"The nutty Koreans."

"The Koreans killed him."

"Yeah, and having you engage in this very public investigation on her behalf is meant to throw everyone off the trail."

"Why would the Koreans arrange to kill Susan's brother?"

"Because her brother was about to turn on her and, by extension, on them."

"I thought he was turning on Cousin Bodacious."

"We knew Attia was debriefing him on what he knew about Cousin Bodacious. We knew he gave Attia nothing. If he had, we would have dealt with it then and there."

"You would have killed him."

"Whatever we would have done. However we would have dealt with it. That's not important since it turned out that Jason had nothing real on Bodacious. On the other hand, he did come to the conclusion that he liked the idea of getting out of prison. His neck was beginning to bother him from giving head to his boyfriend each night. So he cut a deal to work with Attia the other way, to give information on his sister and her friends, the South Koreans. And of that, he had plenty."

"How was he killed?"

"I'll tell you if you promise that we're even. You're going to stop your wife's, ex-wife, whatever, her vendetta against us, for her good and yours. Do I have your word you'll do that? Then, I'll tell you how your boss killed her own brother and sent you off on a bogus quest to find the killer—in other words, how the killer sent you to find the killer."

"I will give you my word that I will do everything I can to have Lori drop this. I would do that anyway."

"Close enough. Jason's cellmate."

"Go on."

"He arranged it."

"Can you prove that?"

"That's your job. I just want to remind you of the value of being on my good side. Have I done that?"

"Not really, no."

He laughed. "Then we have more work to do on our relationship."

"I'll check this information out. If it's correct, I'll owe you. How's that?"

"It'll check out. By the way, you want to hear how this all got even more fucked up?"

"Sure."

"The cellmate was supposed to take Jason's manhood and then kill him. Instead, he fell in love with him. Imagine that. He refused to kill the little fuck."

"Love triumphs."

"Not in this case. Eventually, he made it happen after being paid a tidy sum by your boss through her intermediaries. And for the record, I'm glad Jason's dead."

The other of the two men I had taken down when I was last here led Lori into the room. He also nodded at me. He released her upper arm. She rubbed it, looking back at him a few times as he walked away.

Her hair was disheveled. She was listless, reminding me of April the day before. I could not discern any marks on her face. "You ready to go?" I said.

She nodded.

We stepped outside. The gravel made a muted crunching sound as we walked across the driveway to the garden.

When we got to the car, Len called after us. "Hey, crazy bitch," he said approaching Lori. He had an envelope in his hand.

"Get him away from me, Lock," she said.

He extended the envelope to her. "Take it."

"I don't want your blood money," she said. "I want the DVDs."

He stepped closer to her. Their faces were almost touching. I thought of stepping between them but reconsidered. It was good for Lori to feel the menace of all this. This house, these men, ground women down. They robbed them of their souls. She needed to feel that. She had to stop antagonizing them. "You are walking away from this for one reason and one reason only," he said, "out of respect for your ex-husband. But you won't get a third chance, so take this money and call it even."

"I will get those DVDs," she said.

"That will not happen."

"It will."

Len looked at me. "Her car is over there. Take this." He handed me the envelope and walked back to the house.

*

I followed Lori's car to her apartment in Hackensack. Once there, she flopped on the couch, covering her eyes. "Oh, man."

The furniture was mostly black leather, glass, and chrome. There were abstract paintings on the walls, many of which were signed by her younger self, the woman I had married so many years ago. "Lori, what were you thinking going down there alone?"

"I don't owe you an explanation."

"What was the logic of breaking into that place? The DVDs wouldn't be there anyway."

"You wouldn't help me. I had to do something."

"And you brought a gun with you. You were going to shoot him?"

"I was going to force him to give them to me."

"After what he did to April? You saw what she looked like."

"Shut up."

"You were going to handle this all by yourself?"

"Shut up," she shouted, putting her hands to both ears.

"Lori," I said more softly, "is it so bad to live with this stuff out there? It doesn't have your name on it. How can anyone put it together with you unless they admit that they go to stores like that? If anyone raises it, you can just respond by asking what the heck they were doing looking at that stuff in the first place. And more than that, no one buys these DVDs anymore. The entire porn industry is Internet-based now. It's like tracking down some producer from the seventies to give you back all the copies of celluloid film from a movie that used to be shown at triple-X theatres. It's really not worth all this."

"And what if it hits the Internet?"

"Among the million other amateur pornos? It'll be like spitting in the ocean."

"It's an invasion of my privacy, Lock. Not to mention what he did to April. I mean at what point do you just handle this instead of having the women in your life do it for you?"

"Handle it how?"

She went to the window and looked down at the cars on Main Street. "Forget it."

"Lori."

"It's almost 8:00 p.m. "I'm hungry. You want to go somewhere?"

"I was just leaving."

"I said I'm hungry."

"Call Lloyd."

"I don't want to."

"I have to go."

"There was a Korean there," she said.

"What?"

"When I first got there, before they saw me, I looked in the window. They were meeting with a Korean, a man."

"What did he look like?"

"Dinner."

"Lori."

"Papaleo's, like when we were married."

"Fine."

❧

We were the only ones seated in the back area. A waitress was vacuuming on the far side of the room.

Lori ate eggplant parmesan and spaghetti. I had coffee. "How did you know he was Korean?" I said.

She twirled a long string of cheese on her fork. "How long have I lived here?"

"What was he wearing?"

"Gray suit, burgundy tie, full head of hair, about forty."

"Did you hear anything?"

"I was looking through a window."

"He was speaking to Len directly, not his people?"

She took a long sip of Diet Coke. "Just the cocksucker, not the lady boys."

"Animated or calm?"

"Calm."

"Do they know you saw him?"

"No, I was hiding. When I got inside, he was gone."

"In other words, when you knocked on the door and pulled the gun on Len, the Korean was not there."

"Right."

"Anything else?"

"Yeah, I helped you. Now, you help me. Get my DVDs."

"I'll get the check."

CHAPTER FOURTEEN

I dropped Lori off at her apartment and decided to go to the bar at Esposito's Park Cafe on Anderson Avenue in Cliffside Park. It was a cop hangout I knew from my days on the force.

I waved to some of my old police buddies in the back. They motioned me to come over. I brought them all a round of drinks.

They caught me up on some budget issues that were causing the union to suspend contributions to the pension plan. I responded with a few highlights of my recent woes with Len LeFontant. That led to one of them telling me about a bribery scandal involving Len from when he was a detective with Fair Lawn. I filed that little tidbit away for future use.

Just as I was thinking of leaving, I saw Sam Attia come in. I excused myself and walked to the front. "Sam."

"Not now." He went directly to the bar.

"Isn't it late for you?"

"Yeah, so?"

"One round on me?"

"I want to be alone."

"Sam, come on."

"I'm off duty."

"Just a few minutes, Sam; a drink, come on. What else are you here for?"

He placed his elbows on the bar, leaning in. "Look, I appreciate it, but I'm not in the mood for bullshit. Something bad happened today."

"What?"

He closed his eyes.

"Sam, what?"

"I just spent the night at Hackensack Medical Center."

"What happened?"

"Lorraine Chrysocolla lost the baby," he said. "It came early and had no lungs. The doctors didn't pick it up for some reason. It shouldn't have been a surprise, but it was."

"Oh, Jesus, how far along was she?"

"Seven months."

"How is she physically?"

"She'll be there a few days."

"Come on, Sam, let's take a table, and I'll buy you that drink."

"A drink would be fine, but I am telling you I'm off duty and absolutely not in the mood for bullshit."

"Just a drink, Sam. Come on."

He followed me to one of the empty tables. On the way, I asked a waitress to get us two of his favorite calamari appetizers and a scotch and soda. I ordered a Perrier with a twist for me.

"How is Lorraine handling it?" I said, as we sat.

He took a deep breath. "How do you think?"

"You two are pretty close," I said.

"Yeah. Change topics. I'm back on duty. What did you want to ask me?"

"Now you want the bullshit?"

"Yeah, distract me."

"Sam, we can skip it."

"No, take my mind off Lorraine. What is it?"

"All right, fine. I want to talk to you about two things," I said. "First, I need your help."

"Why doesn't that surprise me?" he said.

"Lori was filmed by that prick Tom she was with a few years ago."

"The former detective, the addict?"

"Right, the one Bodacious owned. It's her fucking him, and somehow, before he did the world a favor and died, he sold the tape to Bodacious's porno company. It's now being distributed by them, and she's declared a one-woman war on Bodacious to get him to stop."

The waitress came with the drinks. Sam poured a little bit of the club soda into his glass of scotch and stirred. "My money is on Lori," he said.

"Mine is on Bodacious. I need to get those DVDs out of circulation so she'll stop this craziness before they kill her. I have an idea how to do that, but I want to run it by you first. See what you think."

He took a deep breath. "Wait a minute." He gulped down the entire contents of the glass. "All right, go ahead."

"If, as I suspect, she was totally high when he filmed her, why can't we say that she couldn't consent to sex, and it was sexual assault per se. So, we get a warrant and seize the DVDs as evidence of a crime."

"Thin."

"I know it's thin. But it gets it all out of circulation and into one place. After that, who knows, it might disappear while in the police evidence locker."

"You want to prosecute a crime against her boyfriend who is dead? That doesn't work."

"How do you know there wasn't somebody else in the room?"

"Was there?"

"I assume Lori will be more than happy to say there was some unidentified man who was there. It needs to be investigated."

"Her identification years later of a man who she supposedly saw while high will not stand up. This is a bad idea all around."

"Fine, what else can we do?"

The calamari arrived. Sam loaded it up with salt and pepper. "How about 2257?" he said.

"What's that?"

"I worked on a few cases with the Feds where it came up."

"Never heard of it," I said.

"It's a federal law against people who film or distribute child pornography."

"Lori's not a child," I said.

"Doesn't matter."

"And how do you know about this again?"

He took in a mouthful of calamari and spoke around it. "Part of heading the Organized Crime Joint Task Force is to work with the Justice Department on illegal distribution of child pornography by organized crime in Bergen County."

"Again, Lori is not a child."

"2257 applies to any adult material that is filmed with actors of any age. The producer has to maintain copies of driver's licenses, social security cards—something official that identifies the actors as overage. It has to be maintained by a custodian of record and available for inspection by the Justice Department."

"So, because she was filmed for what she thought was private use by a boyfriend who sold the tape without her knowledge, obviously no one took any identification."

"Right, and no identification means you can't distribute the video, even on the Internet."

"What about adult DVDs of people on nudist beaches and things like that?"

"Usually filmed and distributed from a foreign country where 2257 does not apply."

"But if a US citizens sell it here..." I said.

"That would create a problem."

"So you're suggesting we sue Cousin Bodacious for distributing pornography in violation of 2257?"

"No, 2257 is enforceable only by the government. What I am suggesting is that you go to the US Attorney's office in Newark and lodge a complaint. They have had an open investigation of Cousin Bodacious for years. This can fold into it. If you're convincing enough, maybe they can even seize the DVDs for you. You got one?"

"No."

"Get a copy and take a look for the notice. It has to be both in the video itself and on the cover. Even if it's just not on the cover, that's a violation."

"Her boyfriend's a lawyer," I said. "Maybe we can get him to present this to the Justice Department."

"Yeah, by the way, nobody buys porn on DVD anymore. In fact, nobody uses DVDs at all anymore."

"Really, I hadn't heard that."

"The point is that this stuff is all free on the web."

"How do you know, Sam?"

"Saw a documentary about it on Fox News." He took a gulp of his scotch. "What's your other question?"

"You said you would not be involved in the Jason Heung murder investigation because it was out of your jurisdiction."

"Right, it's a Bureau of Prisons matter."

I signaled the waitress to bring him another scotch. "But you were trying to get information from Jason Heung when he was killed."

"Yeah, about Bodacious. We got nothing from him, and we lost interest."

"How about this? He gave you very little on Bodacious. So, you told Jason that in order for him to reduce his sentence, he would need to give you what information he did have, and that would be information about his sister, Susan. You were using him to build a case against Susan Heung when he was killed."

"Who told you that?"

"Bodacious's people. I am right about this."

He was silent.

"Sam, there's nothing to keep secret anymore. Jason is dead. The DNA evidence proves it. I'm investigating his murder. This goes to motive. I'm chasing Cousin Bodacious when he had no real reason to kill Jason. Should I be chasing my own client?"

He looked up at me. "Interesting question. You ever hear anything from Susan that would lead you to suspect her involvement in his murder?"

"Is that what you think happened?"

The waitress brought a refill of his drink. He stared at it. "I repeat. Did she ever say anything that might lead you to believe she tried to murder him?"

"You know I can't answer that," I said.

He smiled. "Exactly."

"What?"

"It's a favor to keep you out of the middle of this, unless you want to back into some sort of obstruction charge."

"If Susan had him killed, then she's manipulating me to throw suspicion off her."

"Who knows? As I told you, none of this is in my jurisdiction. Others are handling it. I have bigger fish to fry."

"You're not the least bit curious as to who killed your confidential informant?"

"I told you, not really."

"But what do you think happened, just for shits and giggles?"

"What do I think? It's not out of the realm of possibility that she's using you to build an alibi that she was completely shocked that someone would kill her brother. She wants to be able to say later that she did everything she could to find the killer. On the other hand, maybe it was Bodacious or maybe it was somebody else you're not even thinking of."

"But more likely it was her?"

He took a gulp of his drink. "Not saying that."

"You think Cho's involved?"

"Not saying that either."

"And me?"

"Not the type. If you had that sort of hard edge, you'd have more money to your name."

"No doubt. You know anything about the state of Corrections' investigation?"

"I told you, no." He pushed his chair away from the table. "Are we done?"

"Yeah, sure."

"Good, then thanks for the drink, and I have one more thing to say." He extended his fingers along the edge of the table and stared at his nails. "And just remember, this is the scotch talking, not me." His voice had taken on a monotone I had never heard before.

"Sam..."

"Just listen. I never had a kid. Married for over thirty years. Kept my head down and made it through the whining and complaining, the shrieking, the crying, the insults, the mocking—basically what is referred to on daytime television as healthy and open communication in a marriage."

"I'm somewhat familiar with it."

"But after all that, no baby. And at some point, it was just too late. We were past it. Now we're both getting old. She still shrieks and cries and insults me, but not with the same energy. She blasts me each morning before I go to work, you know, just to keep her hand in. And that revs her up, so she relaxes by drinking her way to the afternoon. In the evening, she eats dinner without me, since I'm usually working late by some strange coincidence. Then, she drinks more, after which she sputters out on the couch. I come home to her lying there asleep with the TV blaring."

"She needs to be in AA."

"Look, I'm not saying she's the worst woman in the world. I've seen worse. And there have been happy times. No doubt about that. But I did want to leave behind a kid. Lorraine knew that. She offered to have me make the deposit in a little cup. It sounded screwy, but on the other hand, I knew it would be my only chance. It would have been Lorraine and her girlfriend's kid, of course, but in some sense, it would have been mine too.

"It was a boy. Lorraine and I agreed that I would have been his uncle. I would have taught him stuff like how to shoot, how to fight, how to not be scared of all the bad things that can happen to people, even how to do some of those bad things himself to other people, when necessary. Stuff like that."

"Sort of like what Grandfather was for me."

"Exactly." He paused. "They said he came out looking like a real baby, fully formed. Just no lungs."

"Sam, I'm so sorry."

"Anyway, enough of this weepy shit," he said, standing. "I'm going to go drive while drunk."

❧

Years ago, when I was still working for the Fort Lee Police Department, I had been part of a drug sting operation at *The Spice of Your Love Life* store at the corner of Russell Avenue and River Road in Cliffside Park. Cho and I had been lent to the Cliffside Detective Squad for undercover work there on the theory that we would not be familiar faces in that neighborhood.

We never uncovered any drug transactions, but I became friendly with the owner. His name was Raj. Once I retired from the force, I would occasionally meet him and go to dinner across the street at the Binghamton Restaurant.

Since apparently no one wanted to buy sex aids in the early morning, the store did not open until 11:00 a.m. I was the first to arrive.

Raj was at his perch behind the counter, which was raised three feet to give him a view of potential shop lifters. He was in his sixties and wore a white, button-down shirt and jeans.

"Hello, my friend," he said.

"How's business?"

"Would be better without your police buddies."

"That still going on?"

"I am responsible for putting more policemen's children through college than Pell Grants," he said. "How can I help you?"

"I'm here to buy a DVD. The category is former girlfriends."

He pointed to a corner of the store. "Go to the *Bitches I Used to Fuck* section."

I sifted through the DVDs there until I found one with Lori's picture in the cover montage. There was no 2257 legal notice on the front or back cover.

I brought it to Raj and asked him to play a few minutes. The lighting was bad. A man who I assumed was her deceased boyfriend, Tom, was standing over her, while she was bent forward, fellating him. Eventually, he reached for the camera and dislodged it from what I assumed was a tripod. He held it from his point of view, so that the viewer could see a close up of his penis pistoning in and out of her mouth.

I asked Raj to freeze a frame in which Lori's face was momentarily fully in view. It was definitely her. "I'll buy it," I said.

Raj took the DVD out of the player. "Never knew you had a thing for old chicks."

CHAPTER FIFTEEN

That afternoon, I made my daily stop at April and Grandfather's home in Edgewater. I let myself in. April called downstairs, "That you?"

"Yeah, where's the monk?"

She came down the stairs wearing a short, green, silk robe. The bruising on her face was clearing up, the swelling almost gone. "I could care less. I have two appointments to see apartments later this afternoon."

"If you give me your new address, I could send a few monks up your way so you don't get lonely."

"Spare me. Speaking of new addresses, this will be my new email." She turned her back to me and wrote something on a small piece of paper. The hem of her robe rode up her legs, and I could see the beginning of her white lace thong panties.

"You know, you might miss this place too," I said.

She handed the paper to me. "You don't give up, do you?"

"Where is he?"

"Upstairs doing the exercises where he waves his hands like propellers," she said.

"Qi Gong."

She opened the refrigerator, took out a carton of orange juice, and shook it. "Want some?"

"Sure. Can you do me a favor?" I said.

"Sexual favor?" she said, pouring the juice.

"Can you call Lori for lunch today? Don't tell her that I'm coming, or she might not show. I think I may have a solution to her DVD problem."

She handed me the glass. "The Korean takeout place?"

"Sure, and you'll come along," I said.

"Like a chaperon?"

"Referee."

She finished her orange juice and called Lori from the kitchen phone. As she spoke, she twirled the cord around her forefinger and stared at her black painted toenails.

She hung up and poured me more orange juice. "All set."

"Thank you."

She sat on the kitchen stool, crossing her legs. The robe fell away, revealing her panties again. She slowly covered her upper thighs once more.

"You doing that on purpose?"

"Doing what?" she said, crossing them the other way.

"So what else do you have planned for this afternoon?" I said.

"Just getting ready for when I find a place."

"And Fletcher?"

"Too little to really know what's going on."

"Even so, do you think it's is a good idea for him to leave right now?"

"Do you think it's a good idea for him to watch his father kill himself in slow motion?" she said.

"Maybe it's a good idea for him to spend the remaining time developing a relationship with his father."

"Hard to develop a relationship with a man who sleeps twenty hours a day."

I closed my eyes and leaned back in the chair, folding my hands to cradle my head. "The point is that you're not solving anything by doing this."

She got off the stool and picked up some of Fletcher's toys that were strewn on the kitchen floor. "Speaking of unsolved problems, what did Pauline want to talk to you about?"

"She fired me as a bouncer at the dungeon."

"Sounds like her. She can get really bitchy."

"That's not the point."

"What is the point?" she said.

"April."

"Okay, switch topics. What are we going to talk to Lori about at lunch?"

"She went back there again, to Elberon, this time with a gun."

"Oh."

"They took it from her, bitch-slapped her, and had me pick her up like a daddy gathering up his little lost girl. So, Len beat the shit out of you. He slaps Lori around for good measure, and I've been less than useless in this whole thing."

She took a few steps toward me and tapped her fingers on my cheek. "Nothing bad is supposed to happen to any woman while you're around. The weight of the world is on your shoulders, and you never buckle."

"Something like that."

"You're a little wacko too, you know that?"

"No doubt," I said, taking her hand. I squeezed it, feeling its warmth and fragility. "Can I confess something to you?"

"Of course."

"I'm toying with the idea of killing Len LeFontant."

"You've had worse ideas."

"I know exactly how I would do it too. There is a technique in the Shaolin Kempo Karate system that uses a tiger paw to the chest to seal the breath, combined with a technique we generally don't discuss that stops the heart cold. It would essentially burst the pericardial sac. The body just shuts down, like hitting an off switch. It's untraceable. In fact, given all the illicit shit going on with that asshole, I assume that Cousin Bodacious's people would chalk it up to some sort of organized crime retribution, maybe even see it as a cost of doing business and just move on."

"He deserves it."

"I keep replaying in my head what he did to you and to Lori."

She kissed me. "Do it because he's an asshole, not as penance for failing to prevent what happened to Lori or me."

"In other words, kill him for a reason that evokes mental health."

"I told you before," she said, "you have nothing to feel guilty about."

"I didn't—"

She put a finger on my lips. "Shhh, enough of that. If you want to go after Len, do it because the world would be better off without him, not to avenge our honor. I'm a big girl. So is Lori. We make our own choices. We're responsible for them, not you. You need to allow us to live our lives. We're not your little female chess pieces to move around a board. We're grown women. Don't turn us into something less."

"I disagree," I said. "Something like this is how a man becomes diminished, at least if he's worth anything as a man. He becomes less than he should be. This has to be rectified."

"Sounds serious," Grandfather said from the entrance to the kitchen. He held a bag of bricks.

"Be careful where you swing that thing," I said.

He placed the bag on the kitchen floor near the pantry and went to the cabinet. "Green tea, anyone?"

He was a tall man with a large girth. His salt and pepper hair completely covered his shoulders. I had never learned his age, though I estimated him to be in his mid-sixties. He reminded me of a laughing Buddha.

I had not heard him come down the stairs. People rarely sensed his approach. His movements had a graceful flow, like water seeping under a door.

"No, thanks," I said.

"I'm good," April said.

He filled the teapot and placed it on the stove. "The key is to heat the water. Green tea is better with hot water. Don't ever forget that. My lesson of the day. Hot water for tea."

"You planning on building a deck with those bricks?" I said.

"No," he said, laughing, a heavy rumbling sound emanating from his massive chest. "Planning on you breaking them."

"Maybe later," I said.

He kept clicking the pilot light. "Later it is."

"Let me do that for you, martial arts master," April said, nudging him away from the stove. She twisted the knob and the burner immediately ignited. "Also, thank you for whatever you did this morning to make that hairless asshole stop chanting."

"They're in the park, meditating," he replied, taking down a mug. "One or more of them will be back in due course."

"Go ahead and spoil it for me," she said.

He ran his hand along her lower back, pressing his fingers into her spine. "This is still out of alignment, here."

She arched. "So, maybe before I go to lunch with your star pupil, you might see fit to whack-a-mole it back in place?"

"Perhaps."

❧

I watched television while Grandfather worked on her. Afterward, he babysat Fletcher while April and I met Lori for lunch.

When we arrived at the So Kong Dong Restaurant on Main Street in Fort Lee, Lori was already there. She was dressed in a plain white blouse and mid-thigh, blue office miniskirt.

After we ordered, April picked up Lori's cup and poured some tea. "Lori," she said, "you should know that I'm making plans to leave Grandfather. I'm taking Fletcher with me."

Lori spread her napkin over her bare thighs. "About time. He's a selfish asshole."

"Stop that," I said.

"He is, Lock. The man never gave a damn in his entire life about anyone but himself. You have this hero worship of him that I never understood. It makes you blind to what he really is."

"Enough," I said.

"While we waited for our main order to arrive, the waitress brought a series of Korean delicacies.

"I purchased one of your DVDs, Lori," I said.

"They're not my DVDs," she replied.

"It doesn't have the legal notice on it that's required under federal law to ensure that the actors are over eighteen."

"I wasn't an actor. It was sold without my knowledge."

"It doesn't matter. The notice has to be there. It's not. So, we can report them to the US Attorney and ask the Feds to investigate. Perhaps even have them confiscate the DVDs for violation of the law that says the notice needs to be there."

"That's it?"

"Isn't that enough?"

Lori stood and said to April, "You dragged me out here on a work day to listen to this garbage?" She turned to me. "What about getting all the DVDs back? How about that?"

"That's what I'm talking about," I said.

"You're talking about an investigation that would make this public. That's the opposite of where I want to be."

"This gets the DVDs off the street. That's what you wanted."

"I don't want it public, Lock. Get it? So of course, your idea of keeping this quiet is to start an FBI investigation."

"It's a better idea than you going to Elberon again with a gun."

"You're an idiot."

"I'm an idiot for trying to help you?"

"I told you I don't need your help."

"You needed my help when they bitch-slapped you for breaking into his beach house."

She threw the remaining tea at my head. I moved to the side, and it spilled on the floor behind me.

"Good luck," she said to April.

"Lori," April said, "don't go yet."

"Got to," Lori said, "and just so you know, I can attest that ditching a man can open up a whole new world."

After Lori left, April patted the back of my hand. "It's breathtaking to watch you exercise such control over her."

I laughed. "Fuck you, Grandmother."

"Did I push a button?"

I waved my hand over her arm. "I can always put some of the discoloration back."

She pulled it away. "So sensitive."

CHAPTER SIXTEEN

When we got back, Fletcher was asleep. April went upstairs to move her things into the guest bedroom.

Grandfather and I went downstairs to the basement. A few years ago, I had helped him outfit it as a dojo just for the two of us. At this point, he was my sole martial arts teacher, and I, his only student.

We had considered using my karate school for these advanced lessons. However, what went on here was a level of practice that was not even for inadvertent public view. Using his basement kept everything contained.

I had first met Grandfather as a child when I was enrolled at his small Kempo Karate school in the Fort Lee business district. My father had insisted I go because at the time, the school bullies were on a daily campaign of beating up the police captain's kid.

Years later, when Grandfather gave up day-to-day teaching to train in Hawaii, I took over his school on a part-time basis. Eventually, I quit the Fort Lee Police Department and moved the school to a larger space to build it up.

I had spent thirty-five years learning from him. At first, Grandfather had taught me how to use my body as a weapon. In recent years, he had taught me how to use it to heal the sick and injured. The two were completely connected: dual sides of the same coin. They both employed the *chi*, the internal energy, the central basis of the System he had created.

We had started with the "external" martial art, Kempo Karate. It was built upon complex, dynamic combinations of strikes, throws, and joint locks, what people generally thought of as traditional Karate. But it also was melded with other, more esoteric techniques drawn from Jiu Jitsu, Five Animal Shaolin Kung Fu and Escrima. He had achieved the highest rank in the Kempo Karate system, a tenth-degree black belt.

But in Hawaii, things had changed. Grandfather had taken his training in a completely different direction. He had immersed himself in the "internal" Chinese arts of Tai Chi, Qi Gong and the Japanese healing art of Reiki. They were the analogue to the external arts and just as effective, if not more so. But their power and practicality were hidden to the naked eye. Trying to understand the internal arts by watching an expert perform them was like trying to understand the workings of a car engine by examining the fender.

Four years ago during Janice's last months, we had all gone back to Hawaii. Grandfather and I had used some of the time to train more intensively with Bette, mostly to get her mind off the fact that we were all waiting for her mother to pass away. By the end of our time in Hawaii, Bette had earned her black belt.

Grandfather had helped me use the Reiki and Qi Gong to keep Janice alive for many months in spite of her advanced cancer. Without those exercises, she would have passed much sooner.

Janice died on the same day April gave birth to Fletcher. April and Grandfather named me Fletcher's godfather. I had not gone back to Hawaii since.

In the intervening years, Grandfather had taught me as much as I could absorb of the internal System. He had secretly told me that, once he was gone, it would become my task to carry it forward. I would lead the System.

Grandfather reached into the basement closet and took out kung fu jackets and pants for both of us. The black jackets had white rope buttons up the front and terminated at the top with a narrow white Nehru collar. The pants were also black. We put the uniforms on and walked to the center of the room.

Grandfather closed his eyes and stood in a wide horse stance, waving his arms in giant circles, inhaling and exhaling in rhythm to the movements. I did the same. It was a basic Qi Gong exercise, used to bathe the body in white light, *chi* energy. It would protect us from injury while we practiced.

After about fifteen minutes of this, he opened his eyes. "Send cold to me."

I side kicked to his knee cap. He parried and executed a chop to my neck. I blocked it and placed my hand on his chest, thinking, *COLD, VERY COLD.*

He slapped my hand away and placed his on my chest. I suddenly felt my left pectoral freeze and fell to my knees. "Oh God," I said, out of breath.

He knelt next to me and rubbed the spot. The cold disappeared.

He helped me up. "I felt nothing," he said.

"Would it help if I turned on the air conditioning?"

He took two steps back and held up his hands. "Try again."

I feinted a punch to his face and crouched into a foot sweep. He jumped over my leg as it passed. When he landed, I gripped his calf, thinking, *COLD, VERY COLD.*

He reached down and placed his hand on my shoulder. It froze, and I curled into a ball.

He rubbed the area, warming it.

"Still nothing," he said.

I stood. "We've been working on this for months, and I'm nowhere."

"You're trying to make the area cold."

"That's wrong?"

"Yes, that's wrong. Don't think cold. Think less warm. One pushes in. The other pulls out. It is easier to pull energy out than to push it in. The body rejects an attack from the outside. But it resists less your pulling what is inside outside. Urge your opponent to push his heat into your body, while you pull in the same direction. That will result in cold, which is the absence of warmth."

He went to the other side of the room and knelt next to the bag of bricks. He piled three of them on top of one another. He placed the edges of the bottom brick between two cinder blocks.

I positioned my hand on the top brick to sense its substantiality. I closed my eyes and started the deep breathing again, trying to penetrate my consciousness to the contours and solidity of the ones below it.

Grandfather knelt next to me. "Take the middle one."

"I don't have it yet," I whispered, maneuvering my hand along the surface of the top one.

"You've done it before," he said. "Do it again."

I raised myself into a standing position and snapped my hip downward. I forced the air out of my lungs as my palm slammed into the top brick. All three cracked in half.

He laughed, placing three more on the cinder blocks.

"Give me your hand." He guided my palm to the top brick. As I knelt, I could feel the familiar tingling warmth, a low-level electrical pulse, suffuse the back of my hand where he held it. The feeling was greatest just below the knuckles of my ring finger and pinky. It was a major spout of *chi* energy. I could feel him focus the flow into a gush of white light, unseen but overflowing.

"Ready?" he said, raising my hand off the brick, as one would a small child's. He lowered it slowly. A feather making its way to the grass.

Together, we made contact with the brick, and, though my hand stopped, I could feel the energy continue through the first and reach the second. "Pulverize it in your mind," he whispered.

I opened my eyes. The three bricks were still intact. I lifted the first one. As I did, the second came apart, disintegrating into red chips.

He held up the remaining two bricks in his hands. "Don't demolish. Respectfully and humbly knock on the door and wait until you are invited inside. Step in like a guest, not an intruder."

"Destroy gently," I said.

"Do the least necessary, and in all things, in every respect, always yield without surrender."

I took the dust pan out of the closet and brushed away the chips. When I was done, he stacked a new brick on top of the remaining two.

"Grandfather," I said, sitting back on my heels, "can I talk to you about something?"

He took my hand and placed it on the top brick. "Do the exercise while you talk."

"You saw April. You did work with her after I left. You know how she was beaten by this monster that works for Cousin Bodacious. He broke her. He degraded her. She was nothing more than a thing to hit. That's the mother of your child, and he did that to her, and I was there to protect her, and I didn't, and my ex-wife is being driven nuts by that same animal, and I do nothing but gather the two of them up and take them back home after he beats them. He gets away with it."

"No one gets away with anything. You know that." He came back and placed his hand on mine again. "Let's focus on the middle brick. Are you ready?"

"Yes."

I lifted my hand with his. I centered myself, closing my eyes, imagining the middle brick, its coarse texture, its coldness.

He let go of my hand. I struck downward and hit the top brick. All three split in half. I looked up at him. "What's the answer?"

His eyes were full of mirth, just the way I remembered from my childhood. The Happy Warrior. He replaced the bricks with new ones. "Find it yourself. Become your own teacher. Take your training in the direction you need to go."

"Because you won't be here much longer to do it for me?"

"Among other reasons."

"But you always come back," I said.

"Soon I won't."

I paused. "Then take me with you."

"You want to cross over?"

"I want you to guide me there, so I will be able to find it on my own later when you're gone. I want you to teach me the secret."

He laughed. "It's not that big an accomplishment. We all find it on our own after we die. I simply have done so before I died. I'm simply choosing what everyone else resists."

"It's a huge accomplishment to come back."

"It's more of a burden actually, like a child being skipped a grade. Are you sure you want to skip a grade? Is there nothing left for you living completely in this world? Do you really need to dip your toe in the next?"

"Yes."

"Once you do, you'll be different, definitely different. You won't be able to completely go back to the person you were. Outwardly, you may seem the same, but inside, something will have changed. You will be on a new path."

"If I am going to teach this System, I need to understand it completely. I need to learn all of it, even this."

"True," he said, reaching into the closet.

"Then you'll take me there?"

He pulled out April's lime green yoga mat and rolled it flat on the rug. He motioned me to lie on it, face up. "I'll show you the entryway to where I go, just the first step inside that place. The rest is up to you."

"Fair enough," I said.

He knelt next to me and rubbed his hands together. "Just remember that when you come back, you will have trouble adjusting to the world again. You need to anticipate that."

"For how long?"

"About twelve to twenty-four hours. After that, you'll settle back in, but as I said, inside, you never will be completely the same."

"Fine by me."

"Close your eyes."

After a moment, I felt a gentle tug as he placed five acupuncture needles in my chest. "You are a fire element, so I am using Heart 1,4,5,7, and 8. I want you to focus on those points. You need to bring yourself forward through them. If you want to do this again on your own, using those points will help you."

At first, I felt very little. The needles were so thin, they easily slipped into the outer layer of my skin without pain. I could feel him twist them every so often, but other than that, there was nothing.

"Relax," he said.

The basement gently came into view. I could see the walls, the closet, the bricks, Grandfather's face. It all seemed natural, until I remembered that my eyes were closed.

The colors began to intensify. They were the same, but magnified, like an over-adjustment to a television picture.

As the colors increased, I felt a suffusion of warmth drawing me upward.

I was no longer in the basement. I emerged into another place entirely. It had no definable features, a place of being, a place to float, completely white and without borders.

I became immersed in it, floating in sensation itself. For the first time in my life, I felt nothing: no fear, no anger, no disappointment, no emotion at all. I just was.

After a long while, I remembered why I had really wanted to do this. The secret I had not told Grandfather.

Janice.

Nothing.

I floated some more.

Janice.

Slowly, I felt her aspect wash over me, the warm sense of her: the slow haziness of her being; the scent of her favorite pineapple candle; the soft shadow it cast upon her face; the lips that welcomed me; that lightness and need I would feel when we made love, the way she would laugh when she came.

I was in just the right place at just the right time. Nothing else mattered. I had no urge to speak. Words meant nothing. I would never leave.

I felt Grandfather tug me back.

No, please, not yet.

Janice.

All at once, I was in the basement again. I could feel him removing the five acupuncture needles. My eyes stayed shut. I did not want to open them.

"That was just a minute," I said.

"Two hours." Grandfather said, stacking the bricks.

I rubbed my eyes. "It didn't feel like two hours."

"Never does."

"That's the place you go?"

"That is where I went years ago. Now I go far beyond that place."

"What was it?"

"Prana."

"That's prana?"

"Yes."

"It's so hard to leave. If you hadn't dragged me back, I never would have left."

"I know," he said, reaching under my armpits and easily lifting me. He let go of one shoulder, and I fell to the floor.

He lifted me again. "You can't stand on your own?"

"Give me a moment."

My arms and legs tingled. I felt unmoored, like I could float away at any moment.

There was so much more to the world. It was no longer a matter of faith. I had been to the other side. I knew beyond any doubt that we never die. I knew that for a fact.

And I also knew that Janice was there, waiting for me.

"Ready?" he said.

"I think so."

He let go. "You feel different?"

I hesitated. "Yes."

Without saying a word, Grandfather pointed to the bricks. He had stacked them ten high this time. He tapped the second and the sixth. I joined him and looked in his eyes. They were smiling at me. His eyes were smiling.

I locked my gaze with his. Without looking down at the bricks, I let out a breath of air and shifted my hips lower, terminating in a palm heel strike to the top brick. I felt it move downward in two quick jerks.

Without checking, I knew that only bricks two and six had disintegrated. The rest were untouched.

He gripped my forearm. "And so it begins."

"My first step," I said.

"As I take my last."

CHAPTER SEVENTEEN

I spent the rest of the night at my karate school. I kept the lights off and repetitively performed the 108 posture Yang Tai Chi long form in the dark.

It had been many years since Grandfather had taught me this keystone of the internal martial arts. I had done the form thousands of times, but tonight was different. I was performing it in the afterglow of experiencing life after death.

Though the room was pitch black, I could sense its every contour, feel the air currents shift as I moved, absorb the energy of every object in it.

I had always thought I performed the Tai Chi postures well. But now I realized I had known nothing of their true potential.

There was a completely different level to this form, a flood of hidden meanings, obscure connections. All the wisdom of the world was contained in this form. I had only to open myself to it.

For the first time, I perceived that the transitions between the Tai Chi postures were as important as the postures themselves. There were 108 postures, which implied there were 107 transitions between them. The transitions were a secret part of the form, an overlooked masterpiece of moving meditation hidden in plain sight. In fact, the transitions were actually their own form, Tai Chi performed inside out.

For the first time, I also perceived that the essence of Tai Chi was that the room moved around the body, as much as the body moved around the room.

The words "Tai Chi" mean "Supreme Ultimate." I was experiencing just that: a moment, maybe two, of the Supreme Ultimate. The art of Tai Chi Chuan was a supreme martial art since, at its highest level, it was capable of bridging the gulf between our world and the next. It could serve as an artistic expression of what lay beyond.

Grandfather had shown me the way.

I took my real Chinese spring steel sword—not Bette's plastic and chrome practice version—from its locked wall mount. I centered myself and began the 67 posture Yang Tai Chi sword form.

As it sliced through the air, I could sense a rainbow of color trailing the blade. For the first time, I realized that the sword's metal vibrated throughout the form. I could actually hear a soundless melody emanating from its tip, a frequency that changed in relation to the postures themselves.

I had a sudden insight of how important vibrating metal was to the internal arts. Grandfather's cedar-handled metal acupuncture needles could heal illness by focusing the vibration of *chi* in the area of the body in which they were inserted. That was a focusing of *chi* inward, to unblock and allow the energy to circulate, to heal. Likewise, the metal Tai Chi sword did the same thing in reverse. It would focus the *chi* outward, through the vibrations coming from the tip.

The sword's purpose was to overcome an attacker with compassion, with the least possible brutality. The highest use of the sword was not to stab or slice an adversary. It was to disrupt the flow of his energy, and in so doing, repel his attack without violence. For the first time, I realized that the Tai Chi sword was actually an instrument of love toward an adversary.

The sun rose. I had no need to sleep, no thirst, no hunger. My mind was racing with new connections and a sense of wonder. For the first time in my life, I was truly awake. The lifelong sleep was over.

⤴

Eventually, Bette unlocked the front door and came inside. She turned her back to me as she retrieved her key from the lock. Her red hair lay loosely about her shoulders. She had on a black T-shirt and matching karate pants and carried a canvas bag with the Okinawan character for Shaolin Kempo printed on the side.

She turned and squinted at me. "Why do you look like that?"

I smiled at her but kept moving through the form.

She joined me on the mat. "Answer me."

I took her hand in both of mine. "I'm leaving the karate school now. You'll take over."

"For how long?"

"I don't know. Grandfather's going to move on soon."

"I know that."

"Afterward, I will be heading the System. You'll need to take on the school."

"I don't know if I'm ready."

"You are. And Bette, something else: your mother—"

She put her hands over her ears.

"I felt her presence last night. It was in deep meditation. I know she still exists. She's not really gone."

"Stop."

"Don't be scared. I'm telling you I sensed her."

"Stop saying that."

"Bette."

"Why won't you stop saying that?"

"Bette."

"Why are you being so weird?" she ran into the bathroom and closed the door behind her. She clicked the lock.

I went back to my small office and waited for her to come out. When she did not, I checked my voice mail. There was a message from Trudy Taylor. "I'm on break. Roy Sokowsky, Jason's cellmate, was murdered last night. Knife wounds, multiple. They're putting me in charge of that investigation too. Speak to your boss about this. She knows something. Get back to me."

I erased the message and put it out of my mind. None of it mattered anymore. I had no further interest in learning who had killed Jason Heung; nor in helping Lori with her DVD issues; nor in any other of life's thousand details. There was a larger world to inhabit. I was moving on.

I walked to the bathroom door and knocked. "Bette, I'm going to change and check in with Grandfather."

She was silent.

I walked up the stairs to my bedroom. As I took off my shirt, I heard Bette follow.

She stood in the doorway.

"Hello again," I said.

She twisted her black belt between her fingers. "I have something to tell you."

"Go ahead."

"It may have been hypnosis."

"What are you talking about?"

"I assume that Grandfather put you into one of his trances, and you thought you saw my mother. What if that was nothing more than hypnosis? He put you under and you saw what you want to see, which in this case was my mother."

I sat on the bed. "It was more vivid than hypnosis."

"How do you know? How many times have you been under hypnosis?"

"Never."

"So how do you know? In fact, when you think about it, hypnosis is a far more plausible explanation than you traveling to the afterlife and back."

"Then why not try it with me, Bette, see what you experience?"

"Because I don't want to," she said, walking down the stairs.

❧

I went back to Grandfather's house. He was sleeping, so I went to the center of the living room and knelt on the rug to meditate.

Eventually, Grandfather came downstairs. He patted me on the back of the neck as he walked by. "Ready, Little One?"

"Sure."

We ate a quick breakfast and went onto the lawn in the backyard. We started with Qi Gong breathing meditation. The sunlight peeked in and out through the oak tree branches. There were two hawks gliding in spirals over the nature preserve just north of the George Washington Bridge. I could hear a car beeping in the distance, then another.

We started with stretching exercises. I reached forward, locking my knees and gripping my toes. We usually began our workouts in silence, but I felt an urgency to speak with him. There was so much to learn and so very little time.

"Yesterday," I said, "when you brought me back, it felt like you were ripping me in two. After I left, I couldn't sleep."

"So, what did you do?"

"I did Tai Chi forms. They calmed me."

"Good choice."

"How did you learn to come back from the sleep?"

"I had Reiki masters in Hawaii guide me. In fact, one of them is actually meditating on our front lawn."

"Franklyn."

"Yes, they're not martial artists. They are a religious order of Japanese Shinto Buddhist monks. They taught me a method of meditation. They guided me, as I am guiding you. Eventually, I could do it on my own, as you will. From there, after a while, I developed the System. One followed the other."

"When you came back years ago, you said you had fully transitioned from the Kempo Karate to the internal arts."

"Yes."

"And that is what I am doing now?"

"Are you?" he said.

"Yes."

"Let's do the Tai Chi form."

We synchronized our movements, and as we completed the form, we immediately began again. A continuous loop, just like the night before.

After the tenth time or so, he signaled me to stand in place, waving his arms in the figure eight Qi Gong breathing exercises. I did the same. We stared at each other, slowing the arm movements down.

Eventually, ever so slowly, he cupped his hands and gently nudged them in my direction. I sensed a ball of fuzzy white energy come to rest upon my skin. Without thinking, I gathered it between my palms and nudged it back to him.

I had not done that with him before, nor had I even heard of such a technique. But it seemed so natural, so simple. We repeated the exchange, like waves in the ocean advancing and receding.

Each time he sent the energy, I would feel something more than just the familiar warmth and tingling of *chi* energy. On a level beneath conscious perception, there was something opaque—a part of him, a signature of his essence—that suffused me.

I heard a car pull up to the curb in front of his lawn. I looked over the shrubs. It was a limousine. "Susan Heung," I said.

"Are you going to greet her, Little One?"

"Maybe she'll just go away."

"Which world to inhabit," he said.

"Maybe I'll choose yours," I said.

"Mine leads away from this life. Is that what you want?"

"Isn't that what you want for me? Why should I stay so limited?"

"The next world is limited, as well. And the next. Anywhere we are implies we are not somewhere else. That is an inherent limitation."

"You want me to stay here, give up all this insight you've helped me gain, go back to the manipulation of the Heungs and the violence of Bodacious and the craziness of my ex-wife and all the rest of it? You want me to just ride the brake with the unenlightened until I die a natural death?"

"If every master who had glimpsed Nirvana immediately abandoned the world," he said, "if the Buddha had turned his back on his followers the first moment he achieved enlightenment, where would we be? He stayed on this Earth for fifty years after achieving enlightenment. Think about how hard that was for him, how painful. Yet, by doing so, he left behind a way that even now, twenty-five hundred years later, offers a path. He could have abandoned the world. He had every reason to. But he did not. It was the greatest of all his acts of compassion. A true sacrifice."

"So, you want me to stay behind?"

"I want you to teach others. I want you to teach my son. I'm bequeathing the System to you, for you to pass on. You have work to do here."

"You need me to stay so you can leave."

"Yes."

"But even if I stay, why not just immerse myself in the internal? Why not detach from everyone and everything and just float around the prana all day and night like you?"

"Because life is not about being detached."

"That's not what the Buddha said."

"The Buddha taught nonattachment. He didn't teach us to be detached. Big difference."

"What's the difference?"

"Nonattachment means that we completely and utterly attach to our lives, but when it is time to leave, we do that with the same commitment and vigor. All the Buddha was saying was that we should not hold on when it is time to let go. He was not in favor of extremes either way."

"But we should hold on when it is not yet time to let go," I said. "That's what you mean by not being detached."

"Exactly. That is why you must stay for now. You shouldn't be detached from your life's path. Hold on for dear life. Live until it's time to leave."

"The first step of which would be for me to go down to that limo and see what Susan Heung wants."

"Maybe; maybe not. But you should go back to your life. Live it. Don't withdraw like me. That time will come too, but not yet. Your path is outward among the world, as mine was once. Mine is now in the other direction. I agreed to show you that glimpse of the next world so you would know what is ahead, so you could teach the technique to a select few as an advanced part of the System. But knowing how to withdraw does not mean you should withdraw. The key to life is knowing the difference between what you can do and what you should do."

"In other words, everyone back in the pool."

He laughed. "Yes, dive in and splash around."

I put on my bamboo sandals and walked down the driveway to the limousine. It felt like I was reentering an earlier era, a part of my youth I had left behind long ago. It would be an act. I would be an imposter in my own life.

I forced myself to remember the voice mail Trudy Taylor had left. Something about Sodowsky being killed. That was significant. Susan would want to know.

But I didn't care anymore.

Stop. Focus. Be who you were, not who you are.

As I approached, the driver got out and opened the back door. I looked inside and got in. Susan was on her cell phone. As she spoke, she pressed a button that soundproofed the back cabin from the driver's seat. She nodded toward the small refrigerator. I took out a bottle of water and poured it into a tumbler next to my seat.

She hung up the phone and poured herself water, as well. "What happened to your appearance?"

"I didn't get enough sleep last night," I said.

"Is that why you are not returning my calls?"

"How did you find me here?"

"Your daughter at the martial arts school told me. Are you aware that his cellmate was knifed to death?" she said.

"I heard. Taylor told me," I said. "I also had some indication that Jaegyu was meeting with Bodacious's people. Nothing I can verify, though."

She poured herself more water. "Perhaps he did that to investigate the murder."

"Jaegyu keeps undermining me with you. He also keeps accusing everyone else of being in on this. What if he is trying to deflect suspicion from himself?"

"Do you have any real proof of his involvement?"

"Not yet," I said.

She took another sip of water. "And you agree that his meeting with Bodacious's people could be connected to investigating Jason's murder."

"Yes."

"And you learned that the cellmate was killed," she said, "yet you did not think to let me know about this important information?"

"I should have."

"Yes, you should have." She took a cigarette from her purse and rolled down the window. She lit it and blew the smoke outside. "What is our next move?"

"What does Jaegyu say you should do?"

"Don't be concerned about Jaegyu. What do you say?"

"There is a pattern to all these events, some internal logic. We just don't know enough yet to discern it."

"Agreed," she said.

"I'll speak with Taylor again," I said.

She stubbed out her cigarette and tossed it onto the street. "The next time you learn of important information such as a suspect's death, you will advise me immediately."

"Of course."

CHAPTER EIGHTEEN

I called Bette. She was at her night class at Seton Hall in South Orange. We arranged to meet at the cafeteria.

On the way over, Len LeFontant texted me. He had something to discuss. I replied that I would be there later that evening.

More of the same nonsense. More playacting. I was so sick of it all.

When I arrived at the Seton Hall cafeteria, I ordered a berry yogurt. I sat in the corner, watching the students come in and out. Their trays were mostly filled with junk food.

Bette was late. I finally saw her walk into the room and kiss some boy whose black hair was combed into spikes made stiff with mousse. I waved to her.

"Hi," she said, sitting down and pulling an orange juice from her backpack.

"Who is he?"

"He's in my zone of privacy. Why did you want to talk? Aren't you supposed to be at a wedding or something like that?"

"That's tomorrow. And it's not the wedding, just a reception—no ceremony."

"So, why did you come down here?"

"I wanted to apologize for putting you through that before about your mother."

She finished the orange juice and began to peel back the label on the container. Her eyes crossed slightly as she stared at it. "No big deal."

"Good."

"If I do take over the school though, will you still come back and teach some classes?" she said.

"Yes, but I still want to transition it to you."

"And what will you do?"

"I'm still going to teach, but on a larger scale. As I said, Grandfather wants me to take over the System."

"Do you have to?"

"Bette, I'm giving you something you are ready for. You will own the school, run it the way you want. You're a good teacher. Don't you want that?"

"You're changing. Something's going on with you. You're becoming different."

"What's wrong with that?" I said.

"You're leaving me behind."

"I'm not."

"Are you going to give up being a private investigator?"

"I'm finishing my work on Jason Heung's murder, but after that, yes, I may be done."

"Are you going to move away?"

"Probably to Hawaii at some point."

"That's what I'm talking about."

"Hey, Bette, maybe you should come along with me. You already understand the *chi*. You're a gifted martial artist. Come with me. Let me teach you how to expand beyond that, to build on it, eventually maybe even run the System with me."

"Why can't things stay the way they are?" she said, her eyes glazing. "I'm going to lose you." A second degree black belt, but inside, something delicate and fragile.

"You're not going to lose me. I'm your father."

"I am going to lose you."

"Bette."

She stood, wiping her eyes. "I have to get to class."

"Bette, don't walk away from me."

She left.

I drove south to Elberon. It started to rain. A gray haze descended on parts of the highway.

I parked on Len's gravel driveway. It was still drizzling. I ran to the front door. The same maid as before opened it and handed me a towel.

Len was sitting in the living room. He got up and placed his arm around my shoulder, guiding me to the club chair. There was a DVD on a small table next to it. "Take a look."

I picked it up and examined the cover. It was another copy of the same DVD I had purchased from Raj. It had a picture of Lori giving Tom fellatio. Under the picture was the tag line, *These White Hot Ex-Girlfriend Bitches are in Heat.* "I've got a copy," I said.

"Your wife has good technique," Len said, "but she could use her tongue better. Actually, my suggestion would be a tongue piercing. They call it a stud, of all things. I'm available to give her instruction if you'd like."

"That's what you dragged me down here to tell me?" I said.

"I'd tell her to start by focusing on the underside of the head. It's called the frenulum. Most people don't know that."

"This is bullshit, Len."

"Relax. Take a look at this," he said, picking up a paper from the coffee table and handing it to me.

It was a photocopy of a letter signed by some solo lawyer. It was directed to the United States Attorney for the District of New Jersey. It was two pages long and requested that they investigate Cousin Bodacious for violations of 18 USC Section 2257 in the sale of illegally filmed and distributed adult content.

So she had taken my advice. After telling me what an idiot I was for coming up with the idea, she had done exactly what I had suggested. Typical Lori: would not give me the satisfaction. "How did you get this?" I said.

"We have people in the Justice Department. They intercepted it."

"What did you expect her to do? You gave her no choice." I folded the letter and put it in my pocket.

"Just tell her that we intercepted it. The letter never arrived. We have it. Tell her never to try something like that again. She's just pissing us off more."

I hated this man. I wanted to kill him with every fiber of my being. All it would take was a simple open hand strike to the throat. He was an asthmatic. It would shut down his airway.

"As long as we have this moment to share," I said, "I just heard that Jason Heung's old cellmate was killed. Any ideas?"

Len shrugged. "Like what?"

"Well, for example, was Cousin Bodacious behind it?"

"No," he said.

"Do you have any idea who was?"

"Prisoners knife prisoners. Fact of life."

"I never said he was knifed."

"It's the common way people are killed in prison."

"Jason Heung was burned to death."

"What's your point?"

"I'm asking you to be straight with me. Was Cousin Bodacious behind this?"

"No."

"You know a Korean named Jaegyu?"

"No, we done?"

"How about this scenario? Cousin Bodacious made an unholy alliance with the Koreans—the real Koreans from Seoul—to arrange for Jason Heung to be murdered and Susan Heung to be financially ruined. So, under the guise of considering loaning her money and investigating the murder he helped commit, Jaegyu is going to screw up the financing he promised Susan through the Bank of Korea, get her to default on the mortgage for the office parks, and thereby destroy the Heung interests. Then, Bodacious will take over what is left of the Heung distribution network in Bergen County and merge it with his own in Essex County. Seoul becomes his supplier, which is what they wanted in the first place, since they are not in the distribution business. What do you think, ringing any bells?"

"I'll give it some thought after I find your ex-wife and have her blow me. I think better after being fellated."

Susan Heung and Henry Cho's wedding was held the next afternoon in the main reception hall of the Englewood Country Club. It was inset among a forest of oak and pine.

There were at least five hundred people at the reception. Susan and Cho were major players in Bergen County. Cho had confided that even in a hall this large, they had to pare down the list from its original twelve hundred.

Pauline and I sat at a far table near the band. There were two empty seats where Grandfather and April would have been.

There were fruit cups with parfait at each of our place settings. Pauline took a spoonful. "What happened to the wedding ceremony? They went straight to the reception."

"They eloped in Seoul last month," I said.

She pulled at my sleeve, pointing to the entrance of the reception hall. "Your ex-wife at six o'clock."

Lori and Lloyd entered the reception hall. It made sense that they would be invited. Cho had known Lori since before I was married to her.

"Be back," I said to Pauline.

"Oh, great," Lori said as I approached. The band was playing, and I barely heard her.

"Hi, Lloyd," I said.

"Lock," he replied.

"Would you excuse us?" I said, taking Lori's elbow. "I need to speak to her."

"We weren't going to stay long," Lloyd said.

"I just need her for a moment," I looked at Lori. "It's important."

She wrested her elbow from my grip. "I want Lloyd to join us," she said.

"It's a me and you alone conversation," I said.

"It's okay, Lori," Lloyd said. "I'll wait."

We went to the lower level next to the bathrooms. She sat on a circular red cushion near the water fountain. "You should know," she said, "I hired a lawyer friend of a friend to send the letter to the Justice Department."

I reached into my jacket pocket. "This letter?"

"How did you get that?"

"It was diverted by Bodacious's people in the Justice Department. Did you really think it would be that easy?

This had to be coordinated. I could have done it through Lt. Attia's office. But of course, you and I never talked it through. You just called me an idiot in that restaurant, walked away and used my idea anyway but fucked it up."

"Oh, God, will you finally, after all these years, just shut up?" Lori said.

"Your way of doing things doesn't work, Lori."

"And your way does?"

"Not anymore, not after you alerted Bodacious's people to what you are doing. Now, mine won't work either."

"What would you have done if Janice were alive and it was her giving head on a DVD being sold to horny men?"

"Fast forward, please."

"I'm just saying." She closed her eyes. "I don't know what I'm saying."

"I watched the tape," I said. "It's one of eleven short vignettes shot by hidden camera. It's not long, and other than the fact that you are obliquely on the cover, it really blends in with all the rest of them. This is one of a hundred thousand adult DVDs out there. What's the difference? It'll get lost in all the noise, unless you make a big deal of it."

"So you watched it?"

"Yeah."

"And it turned you on to see that filth?"

"Lori, I'm truly sorry this didn't have a better ending," I said. "Your boyfriend, Tom, was a fuck up. His fuckupedness even reaches out to us from the grave. Why not focus on Lloyd now?"

She stood. "Just let me give them their gift and leave."

✎

It was later in the evening. Pauline and I had danced and eaten and struggled to keep ourselves awake through the endless testimonial toasts from the local political dignitaries present.

Toward the end of the gala, I snagged an empty set of chairs for the two of us as far away from the band as possible. After a while, Cho joined us. He held three drinks, setting two of them on the table. "Vodka gimlets, for Pauline and you."

"Thanks, Henry, and congratulations to you both."

"Where's Pauline?"

"Ladies' room."

He took a sip of his own drink. "Just love the gimlets."

"Have we stepped into a Raymond Chandler novel?" I said.

"Love the sour taste."

"So, you had the ceremony in Korea?"

"The BOK people insisted that we allow them to arrange it."

"Must have been a blast."

He took a longer sip of his gimlet. "Everything these days is a blast, Lock."

"You getting morose, Cho? I thought that usually happens six months into the marriage when sleep becomes more important than sex."

"Don't put off till tomorrow, etc."

"Then why marry her at all?"

"I love her," he said, finishing off the gimlet. He asked the waitress for another. "Simple as that."

"You two do make quite a team."

"She's a good person, Lock. She comes from an admittedly unsavory family, but she is committed to changing all that. I know you've been exposed to a lot of crooked Koreans, but the vast majority of us are law-abiding, hardworking people."

"I know that," I said.

"My point is that this is not a Korean thing. It's a criminal thing that happens to be emanating from the Korean community. But it could be any community. There are criminals everywhere."

"Why are you telling me all this?"

"Because I want you to know that she's not one of them. She's making a real effort to find her way out."

"Cho, you're my best friend. I pass no judgment on your wife. I know she's not one of them on some level. If you tell me she's making efforts to get out, I accept that."

"Yeah, she is. So, any progress?"

My phone vibrated. It was Len LeFontant. "Hold that thought." I walked away from Cho and answered the phone. "Yeah, Len."

"Guess what I'm doing?"

"It's not the time for this, Len."

"I'm staring at the gun your ex-wife is holding to my face, once again."

"Put her on."

There was a pause. "She says she's busy and doesn't want to talk to you."

"Tell her I insist."

Another pause. "She says she's done talking to you."

"Where are you?"

"The warehouse in Newark. The one on Market Street. You know it?"

"Yeah."

"She drove me up here at gunpoint; says she'll pop me unless she gets the DVDs. She instructed me to call you because she wants you to pack them up for her."

"I'll be right there."

CHAPTER NINETEEN

I made arrangements for Pauline to have a ride home and drove to Cousin Bodacious's warehouse in the bowels of Newark.

The front door to the warehouse was unlocked. I heard sounds coming from a loft that was accessible through a narrow set of metal stairs. There was only one room up there with the light on.

Len was seated at the desk. Lori was behind him, holding a gun to the back of his head. She was still in the evening gown she had worn to the wedding. Her eyes were bloodshot.

"Lori, it's me," I said.

"Took you long enough," she said.

"You been drinking?" I said to her.

She did not look away from Len. "I'm getting the DVDs."

"Does Lloyd know you are doing this?" I said.

"Lloyd and I broke up in the car after we left the wedding. He also fired me."

"Lovely." I looked at Len. "You keeping your cool?"

"For the moment," he said.

"How about you give her the DVDs, and we'll be on our way?" I said.

Len shook his head. "That will never happen." As he spoke, he swiveled to look directly into the gun barrel. "What will happen basically can be divided into two possibilities. One, if she harms me, she will be tortured and then killed. Two, if she gives me the gun now, right this minute, she will be killed without being tortured. That's it. Two choices."

"Shut up," Lori shouted, "and get the goddamn DVDs."

"Lock," Len said evenly while still staring at the gun, "tell your crazy bitch that she is not walking out of here alive today. This ends here and now."

"If you don't give them to me, I will fucking shoot you."

Len looked at me. "I repeat, she will not walk out of here alive."

"Who's going to stop me?" Lori said. "We're the only ones here, moron."

I took a step toward them. "Get back, Lock," Lori said.

"Lori, you've been drinking," I said. "You're upset."

"Just get back."

"Len, what can we do here?" I said.

"She's going to die today. That's what we're going to do here. I should have done it when this first started. My mistake, which is going to be rectified tonight."

We were silent for a long while.

"You know, Lock" she said in a soft voice that I had not heard from her in many years, "this was not your fault. Say it."

Something about her tone reminded me of our wedding. She had worn a flowing white dress sprinkled with pink and blue satin flowers. She had told me that they represented the children we would have someday. Children we never had.

"Lori..."

"Say it."

"It was not my fault."

"On the way over here, I counted how many times in my life I've been raped."

"Lori, not down this road, please."

"Five times."

"Come on."

"I've lived a bad life. I did drugs. I slept with the wrong men. And I know I've given you in particular a lot of grief, but for all the grief I gave you, most of which you deserved by the way, you were always there for me, even when I was a pain in the ass, which was most of the time, and I just wanted to thank you for that."

"Lori, you're all over the place."

"I'm done," she said.

"What does that mean?"

She placed the gun on the desk in front of Len, turned and faced the window. "I give up. Do what you have to do." She lowered her head, mouthing something to herself.

Len picked up the gun and checked to see if it was loaded. I was too far away to lunge at him.

He stood, took a wide stance and positioned it against the back of her head.

"Len," I said, "out of respect. That's all I'm asking, out of respect."

"I'm too pissed, Lock." Len said. "There's a limit."

"Len, come on. We were cops once. We don't shoot people in the back of the head."

"If I let her go, she's gonna come back again. I've dealt with this kind of crazy bitch before. They don't stop. I got to put her down, Lock, like a dog."

"Len, I give you my word, this nonsense will stop."

"You can't guarantee that."

"Lori, tell him."

She was silent.

"Come on, Lori. Tell him you'll drop this. He's going to shoot you."

She tapped her forehead against the window. It made the pane vibrate. Her eyes were closed. She was still whispering to herself.

"Lori."

"All right, not in the back of the head," Len said, tapping her on the shoulder. "Hey, crazy bitch? Turn around."

She turned and faced him, eyes closed.

"Len," I said, "are the DVDs really worth all that this is going to cause? Just give them to her. It's the smart move."

He placed the gun against her forehead.

"Len, come on."

He was silent.

"Len..."

"She pays double cost," he said, "and sucks me off. Those are my terms."

"What?" I said.

"You heard me."

"No way, Len."

"She's going to learn a lesson here," he said. "We're the ones who point guns at people." He started to shout. "The goddamn civilians don't point guns at us."

"And where does the blowjob come into this analytical framework?"

"She has to humble herself. I won't let her walk away from this thinking she got one over on me. No way. I'm going to be number six."

"It's a nonstarter, Len. Forget it."

"Ask her," he said.

"I don't have to ask her. The answer is no."

"The answer is yes," Lori said quietly.

"Lori, come on," I said.

"Stay out of this, Lock," she said, opening her eyes. "I am going to suck you, and when you get real hard, I'm going to bite it off and when you open your mouth to scream in pain, I'm going to jam it down your fucking throat..."

"Lori..." I said.

"Shut up, Lock," she hissed, keeping her gaze on Len. She leaned in, pressing her forehead against the barrel of the gun, closing her eyes once more. "You have just two choices, asshole. Give me the DVDs or shoot."

The room was silent again. Len compressed his lips, adjusting his hand on the grip of the gun, fanning out his fingers and clamping down more tightly. I knew with more certainty than I had ever known anything that if he shot her—if he shot this woman I had loved, who I still loved, truth be told, this woman I had watched descend into the cracks and crevices of her private fault lines, who I had watched for so many years just disintegrate, this woman who had once, a very long time ago, taken a chance on me—I would kill him. I knew that for certain. And life would never be the same.

Yield without surrender.

"Len," I said, "what's the big deal if she bites off the tip? You'll still have eleven inches left."

He suppressed a smile, but remained silent, still staring at her.

"And that's flaccid," I said.

He laughed. "You little fucker, Lock." He clicked the safety on the side of the gun, stuffing it into his pants pocket, and took a deep, wheezing breath. "Okay, fun's over. I'll give you the DVDs for three times cost and I never have to see your sorry, white bitch ass every again." He turned to me. "And I want to be clear. This never happened. I hear that you didn't keep your mouth shut about this, and I will start shooting."

"Len," I said, "if there's one thing I learned today, it's that when I'm around you, it's a good idea to keep my mouth shut."

He laughed again. "You little fucking fucker."

"I want all the DVDs loaded in my car first," Lori said in a soft rasp. "Then you get the money."

He turned to her. "You know your husband just saved your life."

"The fucking DVDs now, asshole."

The DVDs took up Lori's entire trunk and back seat. "We didn't get to deliver too many of them to stores, at least beyond the few remaining in North Jersey," he said to me. "I guess she can get a list and buy what little is still on shelves. Everyone's going out of business. DVDs don't move anymore. It's all free Internet now."

"If only someone had told me," I said.

"But it won't go on the web. I want this over."

Lori watched me load the last ones in her back seat. "You sober enough to drive?" I said.

"I'll be fine," she said, staring ahead.

"Where's the money?" he said.

"Lori?"

Without looking at me, she reached into her glove compartment and took out a bank pouch. She counted the bills and removed a few hundreds. She stuffed them in her pocketbook and handed the pouch to him. He counted the rest and zipped it shut. "You're one crazy bitch, but I admire your perseverance." He extended his hand. "No hard feelings?"

She ignored the hand.

He smiled. "I know why you're upset. I heard you say your boyfriend broke up with you today. Maybe I'll give you a call sometime. We'll have dinner. You never know."

"Len," I said, "can you give us a moment?"

"Yeah, yeah, I've got to get some papers upstairs anyway before you drive me home. Unless she wants to make it a round trip."

"I'll do it," I said.

"Fine."

After he left, I placed both hands on Lori's driver's side door. She kept her gaze ahead. "Can I say a few words before you leave?" I said.

She nodded.

"It's over now, Lori. You got what you wanted from him. That's a big deal, bigger than you know. Guys like that are all about reputation. If you say anything to anybody about this, and it gets back to him that you are talking trash, he will kill you, and I won't be able to stop him. Do you understand, Lori? You took his manhood back there. You can't tell a soul."

She kept staring ahead.

"Lori, are you hearing me?"

"We done?" she said, starting the ignition.

"Lori, did you hear what I said?"

"I did. Can I go?"

"Yeah, sure," I said.

I watched her drive away. I remained standing there long after she was gone, running all of it through my mind. It was over; she had gotten the DVDs, but somehow, it still seemed in play.

"You and I square?" Len said, when he returned. He was carrying a cardboard box filled with black loose leaf binders. "Open your back door."

"No, we are absolutely not square," I said, helping him place the box on my back seat. "How can you even think in your wildest imagination that we would be square right now?"

"Is there something you want to get off your chest, Lock?"

"Fuck you."

"Hey, tough guy," he said, as we both got in my car, "I could have killed her. I would have been justified. She kidnapped me at gunpoint. Legally, I could have killed her in self-defense. Out of respect for you, I didn't. You should thank me."

"You threatened to rape her."

He took a deep, wheezing breath. "She got the fucking DVDs."

"I don't care anymore, Len. Honestly, I just want to drive you to Elberon and get back home." I pulled the car onto Broad Street and headed for the Turnpike entrance.

He extended his hand. "But no hard feelings. It's over. As I said, she got the DVDs. It's done."

"There are absolutely hard feelings, Len."

"Alright, there are hard feelings. I'll find a way of living with that. Can you at least shake my hand anyway?"

"I'm driving."

"Fine, you know she does have a few screws loose, but for all that, she wasn't wrong about the 2257 thing. I checked into it when I read her letter. It's a legal problem with the ex-girlfriend series that we didn't anticipate, and we ..."

"How the hell did you intercept a letter to the Justice Department?"

"Truth is that was dumb luck. A secretary dates one of our guys and she caught sight of the reference to Cousin Bodacious. But you interrupted me. I was just about to tell you the ironic thing. You want to hear the ironic thing?"

"Not really."

"I've decided to pull the ex-girlfriend series completely. As I said, the 2257 issue is a problem with all of it, not to mention that DVDs don't sell anymore anyway. There's no upside. I don't need any Justice Department raids on a Cousin Bodacious operation. She actually did us a favor."

"And all the ex-girlfriends out there whose sex tapes will now remain hidden from public view can breathe a sigh of relief. Switching topics for a moment..."

"Not Jason Heung. Christ, will you give it a fucking rest with this Jason Heung bullshit?"

"Well, I figured in the interest of furthering our renewed friendship, you might answer a question I have."

He laughed. "Whoa, just because both our lives have been fucked up by the same loopy bitch doesn't make us bosom buddies."

"Lovely."

"What do you want to know?"

"Tell me about Jaegyu."

"Who?"

I took the ramp onto Route 21. "Come on, Len, Jaegyu."

He closed his eyes. "What do you want to know?"

"Tell me about him."

"He's a maniac. We want nothing to do with him or his people."

"Too much of a maniac for Cousin Bodacious? Come on."

"Yes, as a matter of fact, too much of a maniac for Cousin Bodacious. Know what?"

"What?"

"He wanted to pay us to kill you, just like your boss killed her brother by burning him to nothing more than a nose ring."

"Did he say why he wanted to kill me?" I said.

"The discussion didn't get that far."

"What did you tell him?"

"That we're not his nigger boys. He can do his own dirty work."

"Are you saying this is racial?"

"Absolutely, it's racial. The Koreans look down on us like the hired help. Fuck them. They don't even belong in this country."

"So, I guess I should be thankful that Jaegyu came across as a racist or you would have been more prone to help him kill me."

He laughed. "Yeah, racism saved your life." He stretched his back. "I get hungry after a good blowjob, even a good almost-blowjob. You want to go for some food down at the shore?"

"To help you celebrate a day well-lived?"

"To say we're square with one another."

"I'll take a pass."

He shrugged. "Suit yourself."

CHAPTER TWENTY

After dropping Len off, I drove to Grandfather's house and let myself in. He was upstairs sleeping.

I went to the basement and changed into a black kung fu uniform. I hefted two cinder blocks to the middle of the room and placed a red brick between them. I centered myself with a few short breaths and reverse punched downward, cracking the brick in half.

I placed another brick on the cinder blocks. If there was one consistent theme in my life, it was my utter failure to protect Lori from herself. I had known her for twenty-two years. She had always been a damaged woman. In truth, it was why I had been attracted to her in the first place: I assumed she would never leave because she would forever need me to protect her.

What I had not counted on as a young man was that her self-destructiveness would ultimately destroy our marriage. The fact that she was so injured inside actually made it inevitable that she would leave me, the one man who wanted nothing more than to help her make her way through all the turmoil.

At least that was my take on it. No doubt, she would have a different view. From the very start, she had accused me of being the cause of her turmoil, and maybe, on some level, she was right. Yet, every time we parted ways, she found a path back. If I was so horrible, why did she inevitably turn to me for help? Probably because there was no one else.

I punched the second brick, splitting it in half. I put another between the cinder blocks and centered myself.

It seemed like she had taken it all in stride, driving off with her DVDs, onto the next Lori crisis. But there also had been something in her tone, her manner, something she was not telling me. I punched downward, breaking the third brick.

Enough of this. I went upstairs to Grandfather's bedroom. He was asleep, as I knew he would be. I took out the antique cedar acupuncture needles and inserted them into Heart 7 and Spleen 6. His hand was warm to the touch. I took it in both of mine and squeezed tightly.

After about ten minutes, I took the acupuncture needles out and dropped them in an alcohol solution we kept near his bed. He did not stir.

I held his hand again and tried to get back to that blank, white place, that formless plane of white light to which he had taken me. I needed to be back there. And this time I would stay. I wanted to leave this world for good. It held nothing for me but pain and disappointment.

I opened my eyes. Grandfather was still in his deep sleep, and I was still with the living.

❧

I drove aimlessly, replaying in my mind the encounter with Len. There was something that bothered me beyond the obvious. *Just like your boss killed her brother by burning him to nothing more than a nose ring.*

There had been a nose ring in the cadaver's nose. But the cellmate Sokowsky had also given me what purported to be Jason's nose ring. It was certainly possible that Jason had been the proud owner of two nose rings. But was it likely?

We had tested the DNA of the cadaver and confirmed it was Jason. So, what possible reason could there have been to add a bogus nose ring into the mix? Whoever did this had to know that the family would order a DNA test and that test would prove it was Jason. None of it made sense.

I ended up back at Pauline's house. I let myself in. The living room was dark. I went into the kitchen and made myself a pesto and turkey sandwich.

I heard Pauline walk to the banister at the top of the stairs. "Is that you, Lock?" she called out. "It's nearly 3:00 a.m."

"Sorry, you want me to go?"

"Come up and cuddle."

I went to her bedroom. She turned on the lamp next to her bed and made room for me. I stripped off my clothes and crawled in next to her.

"So, what was the big emergency?" she said.

"You remember Lori's little porno problem?"

"Yeah."

"Well I just sat in Len LeFontant's office while he almost raped and killed her over the DVDs."

"My God. But almost, right? It didn't happen?"

"No, but once again, I was less than useless to her."

"But she has the DVDs now?"

"Yeah, but come on," I said.

"That's something."

"Paulie, she almost had to blow him."

"But she got the DVDs."

"You sound like Len."

"What else? Come on."

"Grandfather," I said.

"That's what I figured."

"He is really on his way out. He's really dying this time, and I..." My breath caught. I felt my eyes start to moisten. I pushed the words through. "I don't know what to do about all of it."

"I know how close you are to him," she said softly.

"I need to make major changes, Paulie. I just can't go on like this."

"You're singing my song, Lock. So now we really do have something in common."

"Yeah, two broken people working for criminals."

"But unlike me, you can get out," she said. "Cousin Bodacious would never tolerate me up and leaving the dungeon. But you can just quit the blushing bride."

"As I told you, I really can't. I'm in the middle of a murder investigation concerning her brother. What do I do, walk into her office and tell her that the investigation doesn't fulfill me?"

Pauline kissed me on the cheek. "The women in your life always seem to be claiming their piece of you."

"Apparently."

She rested her head on my lap. I stroked her hair

"I like you like this," she said. "If you could only be like this all the time, things would be fine between us."

"My approaching nervous breakdown is good for our relationship?" I said.

"What I mean is that you hold me at arm's length. And the truth is that I usually like it that way for whatever fucked-up psychological reason. But occasionally, it's nice to see what's underneath."

I smiled. "So long as I don't make a habit of it."

"Exactly."

"Paulie, I need to tell you something."

"You fucked April."

"How did you know?" I said.

"Wasn't hard to figure out."

"It was in a moment of weakness. She was going through some things. Len did his number on her. Grandfather is dying. I wanted to be there for her."

"So, feeling such a sense of responsibility, you fucked her?"

"She needed me at that moment."

"So it was a sympathy fuck."

"The truth is I needed her, as well."

Pauline sat up and drank some water from a cup on her night table. "Let me tell you something about women. We know all about your need to feel you are protecting us. We use your guilt over failing to protect us to get what we want. It's Female School 101. They give you a wallet card explaining it when you get your first period."

"Maybe; I don't know."

"And another thing. Women compete with one another in vicious and underhanded ways. As much as we are always writing articles in family magazines and going on talk shows to espouse how collaborative, inclusive and warm we are with one another as opposed to the evil world of men, that's all bullshit. We are more competitive with one another than men in many ways. It's more subtle, but, as I said, also more vicious and underhanded. April has always had a competitive thing with me. Taking you away from me is a massive 'fuck you' to her boss."

"I think you may be exaggerating a bit."

"Really? I hire Grandfather as my bouncer, which is a position that is not so easy to fill at a dungeon, as you well know. She marries him, and he's gone. I have a relationship with you, and she gets you to help her in an outcall situation, which essentially is a way of stealing money from me. Then she quivers her lip and gets you to fuck her behind my back, which is another way of stealing from me. Next, I'll wake up one day and the Maserati will be gone."

"A little dramatic."

"Says the man who's having a nervous breakdown. You need to understand how the women in your life are manipulating you—me included. Until you understand that, you will constantly be chasing after approval which you will get only temporarily. So what's that worth? There will always be another rescue, another disaster that you need to fix. And if you don't, you'll get it right between the eyes from both feminine barrels, the quivering lip and angry words, the disapproval and recriminations, the drama."

"Does Susan Heung fall into the same category?"

"Absolutely, she has you dancing like a marionette."

"It all sounds pretty fucked up, doesn't it?"

"There's nothing more pathetic to a woman than a man she can manipulate. It breeds contempt. The more he tries to please her and make her happy, the more disdain she develops for him, the more of a pussy she thinks he is. A man who always does what a woman wants is just too damn feminine. On the other hand, a man who never does what a woman wants is too damn brutish and cold. He has to be somewhere in-between to get it right, but the problem is that the woman herself doesn't know exactly where that between point is. She couldn't define it if she tried, at least not before he fails to figure it out. Then, she can explain in full detail what he didn't do that she never told him she wanted in the first place."

"Which you've done more than once."

"Don't bring up irrelevancies."

"So what's the answer?"

She danced her fingers on my thigh. "You treat me better for a start."

"You trying to manipulate me?"

"One hundred percent."

"No, really, what do I do?"

She gathered the covers around her. "You man up. You be a man."

"What does that mean?"

"You do your job. You finish this thing for Susan, and then tell her you're out. You stand by Grandfather to the bitter end. You break up with me. Just put us out of our misery. And you get Lori the fuck out of your life. Just walk away next time she has a meltdown or screws up. It'll be better for you and for her. Then, you take up with the widow April until that plays itself out, and then you end that too. You spend more time with your daughter. You practice your martial arts. You live your life without excuses and regrets. No whining, no nervous breakdowns, just one foot in front of the other. Just be a man."

"I plan to be done with Susan after I finish the Jason investigation."

"For real?"

"Really. I keep saying that I only work for criminals, but I'm not one of them. That's bullshit. I am one of them. It has to stop."

"How will you support yourself?"

"I'll come up with something."

"I think I'm falling in love with you all over again."

"Didn't you just mention somewhere in there that we should break up?"

"Sorry, I forgot. Yeah, you're right. We should break up."

"So you are saying that?"

"Yes, but I don't want to be the one to break us up," she said.

"What does that mean?"

"You should do it. Be the man so I can blame you."

"All right, we're broken up."

She laughed. "Gives me goose bumps when you're all take charge like that."

"Come here," I said. I hugged her as tightly as I could. She leaned into me. We stayed like that for a long while.

"Look," I whispered, "just manned up."

"So I feel."

❧

Afterward, I lay next to her, lightly kissing her shoulders.

"It's fun being broken up," she said.

"It is, but I should go."

"There's one more thing I thought of while we were doing our little number here," she said.

"I thought your complete attention was on me."

"You don't get to guilt the female. Only works the other way around."

"Of course."

She sat up, leaning against the pink headrest. "The main thing that doomed our relationship from the start was not April or Lori or Grandfather or Cousin Bodacious. It was Janice. She hung over everything about us in every meaningful way. And she will do so when you take up with April more permanently, and after things don't work out with April, with the next woman. Janice is your unfinished business, and you have to put her behind you."

"I know that."

"I'm going to tell you something that I've known for a long time and never shared. I didn't want to hurt you. It's about Janice. It'll be my parting gift to you."

"Go ahead," I said.

"Janice was bi. She was having an affair with a woman behind your back when you were married. She kept it up pretty much to the bitter end. April told me once. It was another little tidbit to undermine my view of you in some circular way. But I don't know who the woman was."

"I do," I said. "It was Lorraine Chysocolla. She's a detective who works with Attia."

"Never heard of her."

"She was recently pregnant and lost the baby."

"Sad."

"She met Janice through a breast cancer awareness seminar years back, believe it or not. I kind of always suspected something was going on. I just never pursued it."

"My point is that you have this idealized view of Janice that may not be the same as what she actually was. So, maybe you should pursue it because if you do, it will help you see her as a flawed woman like all the rest of us living, breathing females."

"Pursue it how?"

"Well, it might do you some good to talk to this Lorraine chick."

"I was meaning to go to the hospital to visit her anyway."

"You should." She pulled the covers to her neck and sank herself into the pillow. "Got one more thing to tell you."

"There's more?"

"You should be kinder to yourself. There's a good man—stable, generous, and reliable—inside of you. You should stop doubting that."

"This is what you tell me after we break up?"

"Female School."

"I feel the same way about you," I said.

"Hey, I really mean it. You care about people. You raised Bette well. You care for Grandfather. You treated me with respect, far better than I am used to from your gender. You're just too damn hard on yourself."

"But we're still breaking up?" I said.

She smiled. "Yes, but on what an up note."

CHAPTER TWENTY-ONE

The next morning, I went to Hackensack Medical Center. I had been there more times than I wanted to count. I had been shot three times. My arm had been accidentally sliced with a broadsword at the karate school. I had been with Janice here the time her ex-husband raped her and later, for her cancer treatments. There were also the dozens of Emergency Room interviews I had conducted with victims of violence when I was a detective serving under Sam Attia.

Yet I had never been to the maternity ward. In fact, I had no idea where it was. I suppose that said it all.

The nurse at the front desk told me there was no maternity ward, as such. They had just completed a 35,000-square-foot Child Birth Pavilion.

I made my way across the campus to the pavilion. The security guard directed me to Lorraine Chrysocolla's room.

She was sitting up in her bed, reading *Home Design* magazine. There were bouquets of flowers and plants along the air conditioner grating under the window. She looked paler than usual. I could not tell if that was because of anemia, an absence of makeup or both.

"How you feeling, kiddo?" I said.

She placed the magazine on her lap. "Lock Tourmaline," she said, shimmying up on the pillows behind her. "I was just talking about you on the phone this morning with Sam Attia."

"Really?"

"He's ready to offer you a deal to keep you out of jail."

"I didn't know I was going to jail."

"It's not important that you know. It's important that we know."

"Well, I do need a vacation."

"He's been trying to reach you. Where have you been?"

"Wandering aimlessly."

She reached for her cell phone. "Hold that thought. I'm texting Sam that I tracked you down, star detective that I am."

"A trained sleuth."

She put the cell phone back in the top drawer of her night table. "If only I had my gun right now, I could even place you under arrest."

"They tell you when you're getting out of here?"

"Real soon, maybe tomorrow."

"I'm so sorry about the baby."

"Thanks, let's not talk about that. I'd rather discuss the deep shit you're in."

"You need anything?"

"Not really."

"Your girlfriend been here?"

"Becky. She's been here every day."

I reached into my pocket and took out a small gold box of Godiva chocolates. "I thought you might feel like going off your diet."

She took the box and untied the ribbon, selecting a candy. "Not having PMS cravings yet for obvious reasons, but, whatever." She unwrapped one of the chocolates and put it in her mouth. "You look like shit, by the way."

"Just broke up with my girlfriend."

"Blonde with the muscles?" she said.

"Yeah, and she's not available, to answer your next question."

"At the moment."

"On the topic of women in my life, can I ask you a question? It's private."

"Sure," she said, adjusting herself again. She winced as she moved onto her side. "We have some time before Sam gets here to cuff you."

"Did you have an affair with my second wife before she died?"

"Jesus, that's the question?"

"Did you?"

"Where did that even come from?"

"Just something I've been thinking about recently."

"I don't know how to answer."

"The truth would be nice."

She stared at the ceiling and finished chewing the candy. "We did."

"How long?"

"About a year."

"After the diagnosis?"

"Yeah."

Did I really want to go into this? Would it serve any real purpose? "So, why wasn't I enough?" I said, taking a chocolate and giving her back the box.

"I could ask the same thing of you."

"She was my wife, Lorraine. I'm the one who gets to ask."

She kept her gaze on the box, playing with the burgundy ribbon. "Ancient history, Lock. Let it go."

"I still live with her in my mind every day—every hour sometimes," I said. "It's not ancient to me."

"People do all sorts of boneheaded things that they can't defend or even explain later. As I said, ancient history. Forget it. Move on."

"That time she walked out on me, left the school, and said she was going to her mother's, I knew that wasn't true because she hated her mother. I knew she was staying with someone else. But because of the cancer she had pulled away from all her friends, so there was no one else for her to stay with at that point. The someone else was you, right?"

"Yeah, you were too occupied helping your ex-wife with some drug problem, and Janice's daughter was being difficult."

"Bette."

"Right. She must be grown up by now."

"In college."

"Unbelievable."

"She's an impressive young woman."

"No doubt because she had you as a father."

"Why did Janice take up with you, Lorraine, for real?"

"She was overwhelmed. The cancer was eating its way through every organ in her body. She needed a shoulder."

"I have two shoulders," I said.

"She needed a third."

"And you followed us to Hawaii when she was in the last stages."

"I saw her for a weekend when she was in Hawaii with you. It was toward the end."

"I remember her going off. I figured she just needed time alone."

"She was with me."

"Terrific."

Lorraine rubbed her eyes with the back of her wrist. "What I had with her does not diminish what you two had."

"Have you gotten over her?" I said.

"I have."

"Well, I haven't."

She fluffed her blanket. "Lock, I was hurting too when she died. I would see you come by the station to go drinking with Sam. I saw how much pain you were in. The one person who could understand what I was going through after she died was you, who was also the one person I could not tell."

"You took her away from me."

"For a short time, from time to time, but she never left you."

"There wasn't much time to spare."

"Hey, I'm sorry."

"That makes two of us."

She shook her head, staring out the window. "What else can I say?"

"Anyway, thanks for being honest. Sorry to drop this on you with everything else."

"No, you took my mind off my situation. Chose a strange way to do it, but you got me thinking about something else than the baby. That's good."

"So, how you holding up with that?"

"Not great."

"Anything I can do?"

"I'd ask you to help Becky and me make another baby, but Sam's got that covered."

"I never realized how tight you were with him."

She stared at the covers. "You know, seriously, Sam and I have been talking about you a great deal."

"Really?"

"Yeah, can I give you a piece of advice, you know, as a friend?"

I leaned against the wall. "Sure."

"We're going to arrest Susan Heung and all her people very soon, probably tomorrow. You are very likely to be a part of that."

"I'm going to be arrested tomorrow? That's what you were talking about? This isn't a joke?"

"It isn't a joke."

"I didn't do anything."

"You're telling the wrong person. Tell Sam."

"I will. He has enough to arrest me?"

"More than enough."

"Like what?" I said.

"Sam will be here soon, and you can ask him. What he and I have been talking about is I've been telling him to offer you a deal instead. I suggest you jump at it."

&

Sam Attia arrived. Since it was a Saturday, he was unshaven and wore a white T-shirt and jeans. He placed a Dunkin' Donuts bag on her eating tray.

"That's for you, sweetheart," he said, handing Lorraine one of the coffees and a chocolate donut.

"Thanks," she said.

He handed the other donut to me. I sat in one of the guest chairs. "So, Lorraine gave you a heads-up?" he said.

"Not really."

He looked at Lorraine and back at me. "Are you prepared to betray all your Heung friends and help me get them arrested and prosecuted?"

"And if I don't?"

"I'll take you into custody." He wolfed down half of a donut. "I don't want you giving anything away to your compatriots."

"So, I can walk out of here as a CI or in handcuffs."

"Truthfully," Sam said, "I have no real desire to arrest you. But if you don't agree to switch sides and help me as a confidential informant, I will."

"Some friend."

"You and Cho worked for me for a long time. But the minute the two of you retired, you started working for criminals. Not a good indication of your dedication to law enforcement."

"The prodigal sons."

"The pursuers of the fast buck," he said.

"I'm extricating myself from them, Sam. You know that."

"You've been extricating from them for years. It's all bullshit."

"Does the timing of any of this have a connection to Jason's cellmate, this Sokowsky character, getting knifed to death?"

"Yes, it does."

"And Jason Heung's murder?"

"That too."

"Care to elaborate?"

"If I do, there'll be no turning back, so I need to know. You with me or not?"

The family lounge was across the hall. Some teenagers walked in and sat at a table. One of them plugged in a laptop, and the rest leaned over to view the screen. "I still don't get why you think you have a basis to arrest me."

"Really?"

"Yeah, really."

"First, the money you are being paid by Susan Heung to do the bodyguarding is the result of profits from the family's illicit drug activities. I know she says they are winding down their involvement in the drug trade, but they still have their hand in, believe me. So, I can seize all your assets under the forfeiture laws: bank accounts, the karate school, your car, everything. Second, you interfered with the Jason Heung murder investigation."

"The investigating officer, that Taylor woman, has been working with me," I said.

"Surprise—she works for us."

"So, she'll take the position that I interfered, held back information and such?"

"Maybe."

"That's thin, Sam, and you know it."

He stared at his coffee a long while. "Susan Heung got to the cellmate somehow and had him killed. That's not thin."

"I thought Bodacious owned that prison. How could Susan Heung get someone killed like that?"

"Bodacious makes money on the larger stuff, the pilfering of food for sale to the outside and the sale of drugs on the inside. In fact, when they saw I was questioning Jason Heung about Bodacious, they brought in the cellmate to take his manhood. That was your friend Len LeFontant's idea, by the way. Quite a sexual pervert, if you ask me."

"I would tend to agree."

"But they waited too long. The cellmate ended up having a love affair with Jason and all the rest of it; the two of them against the world—that kind of thing. Killing Jason would have been quick, and it would have been over. By screwing around, so to speak, it all dragged out and gave Jason the option to get back in touch with me."

"To inform on Susan."

"Right, he had no real information on Bodacious that would have stood up in court. So, to get me interested again, he agreed to spill his guts about his family's operation."

"But, Sam, if we look at it another way, it all actually ended up hurting Susan Heung, so maybe Len LeFontant wanted to give Jason a reason to turn on his own family. Maybe it was tactical."

Attia nodded. "You're right. That's also a possibility. It's the one piece of this that I don't have a handle on. I've never been able to figure out if the Bodacious people are really smart or really lucky. Things just seem to keep going their way."

"My vote is really smart," I said.

"Mine too," Lorraine said.

"I'm not so sure," Attia said. "Anyway, when Susan Heung realized that Jason was cooperating with me, she knew that the only thing he really had to give was information about her. Bodacious was not going to kill him, at least not fast enough. Now, she had to do it herself."

"You're saying that Susan killed Jason?"

"No, I'm not."

I nodded. "I know you're not. As you were speaking, I finally figured out what happened here."

He half-smiled. "Really?"

"Yes," I said. "The reason I've assumed that the cadaver was Jason's body was because of the DNA test that came back from the company you referred me to. But the problem with that assumption is that you are the one who directed me to them, and therefore, assuming you are trying to manipulate my investigation, the results are suspect. So, the DNA results may be doctored, and the cadaver we think is Jason may not be."

He nodded.

"And the two nose rings," I said.

"Two nose rings?"

"Yeah, that was obviously a screw up. The cellmate gave me Jason's nose ring. But the cadaver had a nose ring too. So, let's assume that the cadaver had a fake nose ring to convince me that it was Jason because it was not. It would make no sense for someone to prevent me from knowing that a dead man's cadaver was the wrong one if he was nevertheless dead. But it would make a hell of a lot of sense if all of this was to convince me that the cadaver was Jason, when in fact he was not dead. He's alive."

"I trained you well, former detective."

"And who else knows this?" I said.

"Well, apparently, Susan Heung knows it. Clearly, she's been playing you with this investigation bullshit. You're involvement is just for show. It's what she would have had you do if Jason was, in fact, dead. She's trying to kill him for real now."

"Using this Jaegyu prick," I said.

"By the way," Sam said, "that guy's name came up in a different context. Something that might interest you that we picked up on surveillance."

"Which is?"

"He's also trying to convince the Bodacious people to kill you."

"I know, and I take it we all agree that hasn't happened yet."

"Doesn't mean it won't."

"So," I said, "Susan is working with Jaegyu to find Jason and kill him. But Jaegyu is working with Bodacious and wants to kill me. My head is spinning."

"Great quality for a detective," Lorraine said.

"Where is Jason?" I said.

"Before I answer that, you need to make a decision. You in or out?"

"How much time do I have?"

"Stop it, Lock. You've become a disgrace to the badge you wore, just like your former partner, Cho, by the way. With this, you can start to redeem yourself."

"Sam, I walked a fine line, that's true. But I never crossed it."

"From my vantage point, you did."

"Well, I didn't."

He crossed his arms. "You going to help me or what?"

I walked to the window. There were two women sitting on the curb, smoking cigarettes. "I bodyguarded her, but I didn't sign on for abetting a murder. If you're right, she used me to help get to the cellmate, to most likely have Jaegyu, or someone working with him, commit murder. I can't be part of that."

"Good, but this has to be total commitment, Lock. No more fine line bullshit. You are now working against Susan Heung one hundred percent as my CI, correct?"

"Fine, now where is Jason Heung?"

"In the prison."

"Where in the prison?"

"He's not in the place he's supposed to be in the prison. We moved him."

"You hid him."

"We knew he was going to be killed, and we wanted to get him out of there and into protective custody so he could testify. But that takes approvals, levels of paperwork, and other bullshit. Before we could get through all that, we got word that the order to kill him had been given by your boss. So, I had him moved. I haven't been able to get him out, but they can't get to him either because they don't know where he is."

"And the burned body?"

"Missing person from the morgue. We burned an already-deceased body and had Taylor very publically find it at the dumpster. We knew it wouldn't hold up, but we thought we wouldn't need more than a couple of days to get him out. Unfortunately, it's taken longer than that. That's why it all started to come apart."

"And Trudy Taylor is working for you?"

"Yes, she's the one who put the nose ring in the cadaver. It was her idea. Who knew the cellmate still had the real one? I had her there to keep an eye on Bergenweld. And one of her assignments was to evaluate whether you were part of all this or an unwitting dupe. At one point, we thought you might have been hired by Susan to try to find and kill Jason. You'll be happy to know that Taylor came to the conclusion you were just a dupe."

"Perceptive."

"So did I, Sam," Lorraine said. "Give me some credit too."

"And you're arresting people tomorrow?" I said.

"Yeah, and we have to get him out tonight for a bunch of reasons," Attia said.

"So just get him out."

"I need to finalize a deal with Bergenweld, and that will take a little more time."

"Why would Bergenweld cut a deal with you?"

"Because I can get him immunity. When the Feds take that place over, and pretty soon they will, that will be worth something. Once I get him the immunity, which I should have by tonight sometime, he'll help me get Jason out."

"So again, just do it."

"It's not like I just make a phone call, and it happens, Lock. By the time I get this going, Jason may very well be found and end up in a body bag for real."

"So what's the plan?"

"Lorraine is the one who actually came up with a way of using your special talents."

"I was watching the *Real Housewives of New Jersey*, and it just hit me," she said.

"You'll bodyguard Jason Heung," Attia said.

"I'll be Jason's bodyguard?"

"We'll get you in there and have you link up with him. You'll wait for word from me. You'll stick with him until we begin the extraction."

"And then we all get out together."

"You will be protecting him."

"You want me to risk my life for that asshole?"

"You want his blood on your hands? Because that's what we're talking about. They're very close to finding him. He's alive now and will be dead very shortly if you don't help me. I know he's an asshole, but who isn't in this situation?"

"Hey?" Lorraine said.

He reached into his bag and unfolded an architect's drawing, propping it on Loraine' leg. "You don't mind, do you, sweetheart?"

"I'm used to being objectified by my superiors," she said.

"These are drawings of the unfinished North Wing of the prison. One of the contractors who won part of the bid was a former cop. I got him to secretly put a loft in the ceiling. It has electricity, full bathroom, place for a cot. No one knows about it because there are no steps or entranceway leading to it. Jason has been there for a week waiting for me to get him out."

"And what was the plan to get him out?" I said.

"Trudy Taylor was supposed to make the arrangements with Bergenweld. But Lorraine and I've given that further thought. I don't trust Bergenweld, and as the investigating officer, Trudy's movements in the prison are too public. I need to get someone in under the radar. That's you."

"What will you do with Jason once we get him out?"

"I'll keep him in the Fort Lee Jail under twenty-four-hour guard. We are diverting resources to this that we don't have, but it's important, really important. With his testimony, we can begin to shut down the drug trade in Bergen County."

"You can shut down the Koreans, but that won't render Bergen County drug free. Others will emerge."

He shrugged. "One step at a time."

"If Bergenweld doesn't turn on you."

"That's not the concern. Bergenweld has nowhere else to go with this that doesn't involve losing his pension and possibly serving jail time. The real concern is that Bergenweld does not have total control. There are likely elements in the prison guard ranks who will accept the order without question to kill Jason on sight, and there are commanding officers who can easily be bought to give that order. It's like the Wild, Wild West in that place, especially in the unfinished wing."

"And if that happens, I'm to step in front of him and take the bullet."

"Just like you would do for his sister, only this time, his sister's people may be the ones shooting."

"Can I bring a gun with me?"

"Of course."

"How do I get in?"

"I'll arrange to have a guard uniform for you, with key card access to the entire prison complex. You'll follow this map and make your way to Jason. Again, once you acquire him, you can't let him out of your sight. You and I will be in cell phone contact. I'll let you know when it's all clear. Then you'll rendezvous with Trudy and begin the extraction."

"And you said he's in a loft above the ceiling. How do I get into the ceiling?"

"There's no real entrance. You'll need to pull down some tiles and climb your way in through an access built in the plywood."

"So I should bring a collapsible ladder?"

"See, Sam," Lorraine said, "I told you he was the right man for the job."

CHAPTER TWENTY-TWO

I spent most of the next day at the karate school mentally preparing for what lay ahead. I sat on my black Aeron chair and tried again to go back to that place I had visited with Grandfather, completely white and without borders. I slowed my breathing and imagined myself floating.

Someone shook my arm. "Hey, you okay?"

I opened my eyes and saw Bette standing over me. She was wearing her black karate uniform and holding a practice sword. Her auburn hair was pulled up behind her in a black scrunchy. "I was meditating," I said.

"Sorry, you seemed to have stopped breathing. You scared me, like I thought you might be dead or something." A younger version of April. *It's like some kind of magic or something is happening to him, like he's becoming a ghost.*

I stood and looked at the clock. It was getting dark out.

"Give me a moment," I said. "I'll be right out."

I closed the door and changed into the guard uniform Sam had given me. I pressed the code for the weapons lockbox built into the floor under my desk and took out my Glock 9 handgun. I checked to be sure there was no bullet in the chamber and slid in a cartridge of ammunition. I took three others and put them in the thigh pockets of my uniform, sealing them along the Velcro seams.

I walked into the karate studio, adjusting my pistol belt. "Show me how far you've gotten with the form."

"Sure," she said. The Tai Chi practice sword was narrow and long, made of shiny chrome over plastic. Bette closed her eyes and began with a circular movement of both arms, bringing the sword around into a gentle slice forward. The red sash on the handle moved in concert with the flowing postures.

She executed slow, rocking movements, terminating them with hard thrusts and slashes. I remembered both teaching her this form two years earlier and learning it twenty years before when Grandfather had taught it to me in a room just like this, on an evening like this one.

When she was done, I corrected her grip on the sword's hilt. Her forefinger and middle finger needed to point forward while the other three provided a stable hold on the handle.

"Try it again. In your mind, make the tip of the sword connect with the tip of your fingers," I said.

"I do that already. I can feel them merging."

"Yes, extend that energy forward. Make it penetrate through the other wall. Begin."

She went to the center of the mat and repeated the large, circular movements of the first of the form's sixty-seven postures. "Why are you dressed in that police uniform?" she said.

"Prison guard. I'm going undercover."

"Why?"

"I need to bodyguard someone who is turning state's evidence. Some people want to kill him before law enforcement can get him out of prison."

She leapt and performed a jumping kick, landing in a crouch and slicing the sword parallel to the mat. "Sounds dangerous."

"Very."

"Why are you doing it?"

"To help out Sam Attia."

She held the sword over her head, pointing it forward, arching up on one leg. The crane stance. "Sam Attia think it's dangerous?"

"Sam Attia's a proud man. He never asks for help outside the Department unless it's a last resort. The very fact that he is having me do this job for him indicates just how out of control the situation is. I think what he is not telling me is that it's almost a certainty that when I go in there, the powers that be who want this prisoner killed will be alerted somehow. It'll be a photo finish to see if they kill him before Attia and I can get him out."

"And when they shoot at this prisoner, it's a small adjustment to shoot at you too."

"No adjustment necessary. I'll be stepping into the line of fire."

She stopped moving and placed the sword back on the Chinese weapons rack. "So why do this at all?"

"Penance."

"What are you talking about?"

"Nothing."

She sat on the mat and began to stretch her arms behind her head. "What if you don't come back?"

"You mean if they kill me?"

"Yeah."

"They probably won't."

"But what if they do?"

I picked up the sword from the weapons rack and checked the tip. We had dulled it intentionally so the students would not injure themselves. I put it back. "If I die, you will not only take over the school, but also devote yourself to promoting the System. It will be your shared responsibility with all the other black belt masters around the world who head the eighteen schools that teach our art. You'll be one of them."

"What about Grandfather? He created the System."

"He's in the process of leaving this world. Maybe a day or two at most and he'll be gone. It's up to the rest of us now."

"I'm nineteen years old," she said, staring down at the mat. "I won't be able to take that on."

"Not just that, but also when April has a meltdown and Lori does something hopelessly self-destructive and all the rest. That too."

"I'd become you."

"Right," I said.

"Why?"

"There's no one else."

"But as I said, I'm not ready."

"No one is ever ready, Bette. People grow up when they have to, whether they are ready or not, and with the exception of Grandfather, people die before they're ready too. Life doesn't wait."

She walked to the water fountain and filled two cups, handing one to me. "You'll be careful though, right? Really careful?"

"Yes, I'll definitely try not to let them kill me."

She drank the water and threw away her cup. "But even so, if someone shoots at this guy, you'll step in front to take the bullet?"

"That's my job."

❧

Later that evening, I was driven by an off-duty Fort Lee cop to a side street near the gate to the prison. Attia had supplied me with a lieutenant's rank and the corresponding ID. He had used the picture from my old police detective's personnel file.

I made my way in without incident and headed toward the new construction at the North Wing. I had to swipe my card a few times through the various checkpoints, but Bergenweld had ensured that I would have an all-access pass to the prison. Of course, that also meant someone with knowledge of what was about to happen might very easily track my movements. It was a matter of which side would get its act together more quickly, Attia or Susan Heung.

Before leaving, I had memorized the map Sam had given me and destroyed it. It showed a part of the complex that was vacant and under renovation. Sam had highlighted a section on the perimeter of the other side of the prison from the main entrance.

As I went down two floors to the basement level, the smell of gasoline became pronounced. I came to a number of heavy, cast-iron-barred doors. As Attia had instructed, I went to the second one on the left and used the master card to open it.

I glanced down the hallway. The walls were made of cinder block painted green. I unfolded the portable ladder from my bag and took down three ceiling tiles. They were moist, and the edges crumbled in my hand.

There were two sliding locks in the wooden panel above the drop ceiling. I opened them and peered inside. "Jason," I said.

Nothing.

"Sam Attia sent me."

I could hear him next to the opening. "Who is that?"

"Lock Tourmaline."

"I thought Attia was sending the chick guard."

"She'll be along. For now, it's just me."

"What are you here for?" he said.

"To protect you."

"Attia sent my sister's bodyguard to protect me?"

"Your sister doesn't know I'm here."

"Yeah, sure."

"Look, I'm exposed out here," I said, reaching up. "Take my hand and help me get inside."

He pulled me through the opening. Once inside the loft, I pulled the ladder through and replaced the ceiling tiles as best I could.

The loft was illuminated with a small lantern. There was a refrigerator in the corner near a prison-issue cot. Along the far wall, there was a pile of books and a television set with ear buds plugged into the side.

Jason was thinner than I remembered. He had grown a short beard. "So, Attia sent you?" he said. There was a putrid smell in the air that I could not identify.

"Yeah, I'm to bodyguard you until he's ready to get you out."

"Which will be when?"

"Soon, I don't know."

"Days, weeks, months, what?"

"Should be within the hour. Everything should be set by now."

"About time," he said, taking a small box of cereal from the cardboard box behind the television.

"Is there anything you need to take with you?"

"No."

"Then we wait."

He turned the television channel to the local news. He sat on one of the adjoining chairs and inserted an ear bud in one ear, eating cereal. The television picture was filled with the usual crashes and disasters.

After a while, Sam called me on the cell. "Prepare to commence extraction in ten minutes."

"Affirmative," I said.

"Where are we going?" Jason said.

"Not telling."

"I can't believe Attia sent you."

"Amazes me too, actually," I said.

Jason turned off the television. "We need to do something before we leave."

"We're not deviating," I said. "Once we get word, we make a straight line out of here."

"Just listen. My cellmate, Roy Sokowsky—I want to get him out too."

"You'll need a body bag."

"What?"

"Your sister wanted to kill you, but she settled for him. He was the only one she could get her hands on."

"Susan killed Roy?"

"Her Korean friends did. They were trying to find you for a family reunion. Your cellmate was apparently less than helpful in directing them to where you were."

"Fuck."

I tossed him my bag. "There's clothes in here. Put them on."

He pulled the clothing out. "A guard's uniform?"

"And weapons in the side pockets. Do it. We're going to go looking for you."

Once he was done, I called Sam Attia on my cell phone. "Ready."

"Commence extraction."

I hung up and turned to Jason. "Let's go."

I slid out the ceiling tiles and extended the ladder to the hallway. I climbed down first and, when I was sure the coast was clear, signaled for Jason to join me. I replaced as many of the tiles as I could and folded the ladder again. I ditched it under some construction materials.

We walked down the hallway. I heard movement around the corner. I guided him the other way and stopped. There were faint sounds coming from that direction, as well.

"Follow me," I said. We went around another corridor. We ended in a large room with no windows and walls made of floor-to-ceiling, green-painted cinder block. I closed the door behind us.

"What is this?" Jason said.

"It's being built for the electrical junction boxes. It's pretty solid. Even has a steel-reinforced door." I pulled out my cell phone and speed dialed Sam. "Status report," I said.

"Proceed," Sam answered.

"We had to forgo alternative locations A and B. We're in alternative location C."

"Acknowledged. I'll let her know."

I closed the door and went to the far corner of the room, sitting cross-legged.

"What are you doing?" he said.

"Waiting." I took a deep breath and closed my eyes, letting my mind reach out to feel the contours of the room, its dynamics.

"For the chick guard?"

"Yes."

I listened to the slight static from a loose wire in the lighting fixture and the apnea in Jason's breathing. I sensed a faint coldness emanating from the walls and heard a soft dripping behind one of them, a leak that might have meant condensation from one of the pipes.

An alarm went off.

CHAPTER TWENTY-THREE

I opened my eyes. The room had darkened and the lighting turned red. There was a claxon blaring in the background, and over it a computerized voice said, "Lockdown, lockdown. Inmates, back away from the door and show your hands. Lockdown, lockdown..."

Jason was standing near the door. "Nice of you to wake up," he said. "What now?"

"We wait."

"You think by having prison guard uniforms on, we'll just waltz out of here? You think they're that stupid?"

"Listen to me," I said. "You have to do what I say, exactly to the letter. Can you do that, asshole?"

He stared at me. The claxon was unrelenting. I tried to purge myself of the sound.

"Do what?" he said.

"Take orders."

"From you?"

I stood, joining him at the door. "Yeah, for example, go the fuck to the back of the room now."

"Why?"

"If things start to go wrong, I want them to attack me, not you. It's far easier to deal with a direct attack on me than to protect you and me at the same time."

Jason went to the back of the room. He took out his gun and checked the clip.

There were three quick bangs on the door.

I banged back twice.

Another three bangs.

I opened it. Trudy Taylor was there wearing a full Lexan face mask and black jacket and pants. She propped her automatic weapon on her hip with the barrel pointed upward. "You have him?" she said.

"Yes."

She glanced inside the room, saw Jason and motioned to him. "Let's go, you."

We had known they might be monitoring our movements. There was no way to avoid it. The plan was to wait until they declared the inevitable prison break and then start looking for ourselves. We would become nothing more than three more guards responding to the emergency.

We started walking. The claxon got louder. I put it out of my mind and turned, walking backward a few steps to see if anyone was following us. Nothing.

In the distance, I heard four small, metallic sounds. I surmised they were the magnetic saucers on which they had placed plastique explosive. It was followed by a series of loud pops.

"I assume you know the way out of here?" Jason said.

"Quiet," Trudy replied.

A group of eight guards came toward us. Trudy motioned down the hallway. "Prisoner is trapped in the ceiling loft back there. We're setting up a perimeter."

"Let's go," one of them said to the others.

As they passed, the last one glanced at Jason.

"Hold on." He stopped and lowered his gun. The rest kept going for a few steps before they realized something was happening.

"Trudy, go," I shouted.

She grabbed Jason by the shoulder and dragged him in an all-out run the other way down the hall.

The first guard aimed his weapon at me. "Out of the way."

I put my weapon on the floor. "Don't shoot. I'll stand down."

The first guard turned to the seven others and signaled them to go around me. That was all I needed. One moment of distraction.

I had envisioned this dozens of times in my meditation earlier in the day. I had not known how, of course, but I had a strong sense that it would come to something like this. And if it did, I would just need that one moment.

Disarming myself was the bait and switch. They had no idea how much a handgun was actually a hindrance in close quarters like this. Now I could go all out, in every direction, without the imbalance of even a short-barreled gun.

Help me, Janice.

I lowered my stance, gathering my energy, drawing in the white light, suffusing it within me, pulsating, limitless. The light brightened, and I felt my body bathed in it. They could not see it of course. It was mine alone.

I took another breath, and the energy suddenly ramped up, gushing outward. A fountain of *chi*. I breathed it in, yin and yang, centered and balanced.

Alive. Completely alive.

My moment.

I took one short step forward and placed my hands on the first guard just as he was turning back in my direction. I positioned my open palms against his Kevlar chest plate. He instinctively moved backward, but I followed, hooking his ankle and throwing him off balance. He landed on the floor.

I followed him down, expelling my breath and sinking my consciousness into his chest.

Pull the heat out. No pushing this time. Pull.

Cold, very cold, extremely cold.

He screamed. Two others grabbed me, and I wrapped my hands around their thighs. *Cold, very cold, extremely cold.* I heard one of them gasp and the other try to shoo me away like a bee, but again, I went with the movement. It looked like a push-hands exercise in the Tai Chi practice mode. No resistance.

But this was not practice, and I was not pushing their hands, but pulling their heat. I was sucking it out of them, out of the unseen cracks and crevices of their beings.

One fainted, and the other dropped his weapon and gripped his chest plate, rubbing at it furiously, falling backward into the others behind him. They became jumbled, stepping over one another, off balance.

One of them leveled his gun at me, shouting, "Clear, gentlemen, I'm taking the shot."

I hit the barrel with a crane's wing, nudging it toward the ceiling. The shot went wild.

He pulled his weapon away and moved around his comrade, lowering it at my face again. He had an open shot now, and I was out of position.

A twinge of panic. There were too many of them. A sea of black body armor.

Go external.

The Kempo Karate.

I spun around and cross-stepped sideways, briefly moving out of his line of fire, landing an elbow against his faceplate. His head snapped back. I ran my other hand down his thigh, feeling for the point where the front and back bulletproof leg plates met, a gap in the armor.

I executed a low wheel kick directly at that spot, driving my toes into the muscle. His leg buckled, and as he went down, I maneuvered the barrel of his gun over his shoulder to throw him completely off balance. He landed on the floor. I followed, smashing a knee onto his shoulder for stability and a straight reverse punch to his face plate. Like breaking bricks.

The clear Lexan spider-webbed. I punched again, full force, and this time, my hand made it through, smashing his nose. He let go of the gun and covered his face with both hands.

Another lunged at me with a black-handled, aluminum baton. I parried with an inside block, allowing the thrust to carry him forward. As he slid past me, I shot a rising elbow under his chin. It did no good because I hit his protective helmet strap.

But the beauty of Kempo Karate was it allowed for error, each movement creating an opening for a dozen more, an unending spiral of possible moves and counters, ceaseless and expressed in a spare, compact series of interlocking strikes and holds. It was virtually unstoppable when performed at maximum intensity and speed.

He instinctively pulled his arm back to regain balance. I kept the movement going, bending his elbow backward. I reached under his shoulder and interlaced the fingers of both my hands, locking that arm, twisting it further behind him. No armor in the world could protect him from the basic inability of his shoulder joint to allow his arm to move all the way over his head and behind his back.

I expelled my breath and torqued the arm down as hard as I could. I felt the joint tear as he fell.

I was over the hump. Someone who had never been in a real fight, with real stakes, could not know that feeling. In a true life-and-death struggle, a man could only prevail over his opponent if he believed he would win. The struggle was won or lost, always and forever, in his heart. The Supreme Controller. I had decided I would win. It was definite and certain.

Go internal.

Another guard moved his gun into position. I gently placed two hands on his chest and imagined heat being sucked out.

He kept coming at me, swinging the butt of his gun at my head.

Just as his weapon was about to make contact, I ducked under it. He brought it around for another strike.

Icy cold, freezing cold.

"What the fuck?" he shouted, dropping the gun.

I placed my other hand on his lower abdomen and nudged my energy forward, visualizing my hands as reverse magnets, repelling him. I had never done anything like that before.

Become your own teacher.

He didn't just fall backward; he flew into the wall, arms and legs whipping back and forth, expelling the *chi* I had somehow generated.

External again.

I waded into the tangle of limbs. A hand holding a pistol. I grabbed the slide and twisted the gun against a forefinger, breaking it. A man bent over. I reached into one of the pockets on his holster belt and dislodged a knife. A foot arced toward my shoulder. I grabbed it and sliced the Achilles tendon. Another hand seized my thigh. I sliced into the forearm.

I swept the leg out from under another guard. As he fell, I gripped his helmet and lifted it, exposing his neck. I chopped at his Adam's apple, temporarily cutting off his breath.

Another aimed his handgun at me. I slapped my hands together off center, making contact simultaneously with the inside of his wrist and the back of the same hand. As it bent, I dislodged the gun from his grip and swung the butt upward under his helmet just below the chin strap. His head snapped back, and he went down. A guard next to him kicked at my groin. I twisted away and grabbed his foot, increasing its momentum until his whole body was momentarily lifted off the ground. As he came down, I double punched where the armor terminated at the side of his ribs. It knocked the breath out of him, and he crumpled to the floor.

A few of the guards lifted their hands in surrender. I took their weapons and ordered them to place their palms against the wall. I pointed a rifle at the others. Most were groaning and gasping for air. I took each of their weapons, as well.

I used the plastic handcuffs to restrain them. Once I was done, I looked down the hallway. Trudy and Jason were long gone.

જ

I moved the guards into the room Jason and I had just vacated. Since this was a prison, I was able to lock it from the outside, and they could not unlock it from the inside.

I made my way to the main complex. My ID cards swiped through each of the checkpoints.

I reached Lt. Bergenweld's office. His administrative assistant was typing something on an old-style computer. The monitor took up half her desk.

She looked up. "He's with someone, Lieutenant. There's a partial lockdown in progress."

I opened the door to Bergenweld's office.

"Excuse me..." the administrative assistant said.

Lt. Bergenweld was shouting into the phone. Lt. Attia was standing next to him. He nodded at me when I entered.

"Jason out?" I said.

Bergenweld hung up the phone. "Who's this?"

I took off my mask.

Bergenweld stared at me. "Susan Heung's driver?"

"And so much more," I said.

He turned to Lt. Attia. "I called off the lockdown."

"We need to get out of here now," Lt. Attia replied.

"Trudy and Jason?" I said.

"At the perimeter checkpoint," Lt. Attia said, "you and I need to pick them up and go."

Bergenweld held up a red, plastic swipe card and handed it to Lt. Attia. "The reset of the system will take a while," Bergenweld said. "None of the outer gates in and out of this facility will work with your cards. Use this one."

Attia nodded. "Let's go."

I turned to Bergenweld. "I locked a bunch of Rapid Response Team prison guards in the electrical junction room in the unfinished area. They can't get out."

"I'll take care of it," he said.

"And by the way, I think we should call off the search for Jason Heung's missing cadaver."

"Go fuck yourself," he muttered.

CHAPTER TWENTY-FOUR

We picked up Trudy and Jason at the checkpoint and drove Trudy to her car. It was parked a few miles away in a strip mall.

Sam drove Jason and me north on the New Jersey Turnpike to the Fort Lee Police Station. He placed Jason in a solitary cell and assigned two uniforms to stand guard over him.

He walked me to my car.

"When is stage two?" I said.

"I'll be in touch."

❧

I went back to the karate school. The lights were out. I fell into bed fully clothed and slept.

Early the next morning, I was woken by the phone. I checked the Caller ID. It was Attia. "Yeah, Sam."

"Stage two."

"Shouldn't we have done this last night?"

"Yeah, we should have. Feel free to write a letter to the Chief after this is all over about your disappointment in how he staffs Strike Force operations."

"You've been up all night?"

"Plenty of time to sleep when we're dead. Get going."

I drove to Susan's townhouse in Cliffside Park. The weather was crisp. There was a heavy humidity in the air. The sun was obscured by the clouds.

I rang the bell.

Cho answered. "You look like shit," he said.

"Come out for a second," I said. "We need to talk."

The townhouses were located on a dead end adjacent to the Palisadium. There was a small path that led to a lookout platform. The Hudson River was below, and beyond that, the Manhattan skyline.

"What's wrong?" he said.

"Attia contacted me. There's word that an attempt on Susan's life is about to occur."

"How credible?"

"Very; where is she?"

"Inside."

"We need to get her to a secure location."

⚘

Susan was in her study. Cho knocked and we both entered. She was on the phone. She placed her palm over the receiver and said, "Are you aware of activity at the East Jersey Prison last night?"

"What sort of activity?"

"A prisoner trying to escape."

"Sam Attia just informed me they have a credible source that there is about to be an attempt on your life. I assume the two may be connected."

She leaned back in her chair. "What does one have to do with the other?"

"I don't know. I suggest you pack some things. We need to get you to a secure location."

"Is this necessary?" she said.

"At least temporarily, until we sort it out." I turned to Cho. "Can you bring the SUV around, while I keep an eye on her here?"

"Shouldn't we reverse that?" he said.

"I want to stay close to her," I said.

"Fine."

After Cho left, Susan packed a bag. I carried it outside. We stood by the door, and I positioned myself in front of her as a shield. Normally, I would have insisted she stay inside to minimize the ability of someone to target her. But this time, my job was to get her out of the townhouse, to lead her into the lion's den, so to speak.

"How have you been faring?" Susan said from behind me.

"Grandfather isn't doing too well."

"I'm sorry to hear that."

"Thanks. Where's Jaegyu?"

"At the prison," she said. "He is the one who called me."

"What's he doing at the prison?"

"Don't concern yourself with that."

Cho pulled the SUV up to the front steps of the townhouse. He turned off the engine and rolled down the window. "Let's go."

Three police cruisers drove up the block and came to a halt in front of us. Sam Attia got out first and flashed his badge. "Susan Heung, we have a warrant for your arrest."

"Sam," Cho said, getting out of the SUV, "what are you doing?"

Attia placed handcuffs on her.

Cho grabbed Sam's arm. "She's done nothing wrong, Sam."

Sam shrugged Cho off. "If you touch me again, former Detective Cho, I'll have you arrested for obstruction."

Attia handed her off to one of the female officers. Susan stared at me as the officer guided her into the backseat of the cruiser. The officer put a hand on Susan's head to prevent her from banging it on the car roof and closed the door. Susan continued to stare at me through the window as the car drove off.

Cho and I followed her to the police station in the SUV. It had started to rain, and the beaded water on the windshield distorted the image of red sirens.

"What just happened?" Cho said.

I was silent.

"I have to call our lawyer," he said, dialing his cell phone. He left a voice mail.

Our small caravan got onto Route 67. We came to a red light, but the police cars went through it. Cho followed.

He tapped on the steering wheel. "You set her up," he said.

"Yes."

"So, you lied to her."

"I did."

He looked at the slick road straight ahead. "How could you betray her like this?"

"Jason Heung is alive, Cho."

"He's dead."

"I saw him."

"Where is he?"

"Fort Lee Jail, ready to turn state's evidence against Susan, who by the way, was in some sort of unholy alliance with Jaegyu to kill her brother before he could testify against her."

"No."

"She's an accomplice to attempted murder. I didn't betray her. She betrayed me, and you for that matter. She used me to make it appear that she was looking for Jason's murderer, and all the while, she was the one trying to kill him. That's some sick shit."

"I don't believe it," he said.

"Think about this. Who hired me to investigate Jason Heung's murder?"

"Susan did," he said.

"No, who hired me?"

He paused. "I did."

"Right, you called me, not her. She didn't know you were calling me, did she?"

"No, there were a lot of things going on that night. I took it upon myself to get you involved on her behalf."

"Exactly, and once I was in, she couldn't instruct me to stand down without raising suspicion. So she kept me in, but on a short leash, always being watched by Jaegyu, always asking for me to keep her apprised. In fact, as long as I wasn't really finding anything about the real killer, but was off on the Cousin Bodacious tangent, it actually helped her to have me involved. It created misdirection while she went after Jason."

"I knew nothing about that," he said.

"I knew you weren't part of this mess. You were being sucked into it without knowing. I think Attia knows it too."

"I just married that woman, Lock. I am part of this mess."

"So, you do what you need to do to help her fight the charges. That's expected. To that extent, you will be involved, but it will be from outside, not inside, a jail cell."

"We have good lawyers."

"I know you do."

The police cars turned onto Main Street. We followed. "Congress is out for good, I suppose," he said.

"Maybe; I don't know. For now, you need to get Susan out on bail."

I sat with Cho in the lobby of the police station while they processed her. He spent most of the time on the phone with their attorney, discussing how to make bail.

After that, we waited. Eventually, he gripped my forearm. "You can take off."

"Okay," I said, "I suppose I'm fired, right?"

"It is exceedingly likely that she will not want to employ you as her bodyguard after this. You're her enemy now. You know that."

"I do."

"And watch yourself. It won't come from me. I won't be a part of it. I promise that. In fact, if I hear of anything, I'll do everything I can to stop it. I'll even warn you if I can. You're still my best friend, Lock."

"And you're mine."

"You know who I'm talking about?"

"I do."

"I'm sorry it worked out this way."

"So am I."

"Watch your back."

"Always do."

☙

I got in my car and called April. "It's me," I said.

"He's sleeping. So is the munchkin."

"What's the plan?"

"The celebration is taking place tomorrow."

"So, tomorrow's the day?" I said.

"It is."

I hung up and called Bette. "You free tomorrow to come to Grandfather's house?"

"Sure, why?"

"Tomorrow he's going to die."

CHAPTER TWENTY-FIVE

That afternoon, I parked in front of Grandfather's house. There were more than a dozen monks sitting on the front lawn, chanting softly. A small crowd had gathered to watch them. There were two teenagers at the far end of the group, pushing each other and laughing. Every so often, they called out obscenities to Franklyn, who was kneeling on the grass meditating.

I joined the teenagers. "What's so funny?"

The shorter one had a blond crew cut. He was holding a brown paper bag, which he wrapped closed as I approached. "Nothing."

I glanced at the other one. He was overweight and wore a T-shirt outside his jeans. It had a picture of an electric guitar dripping red blood. "You a cop?" he said.

"These men are praying," I replied. "You shouldn't be laughing it up."

"Okay," the smaller one said. "We'll be good."

"Let's shake on it," I said.

"Yeah, sure."

I closed my grip and pulled the warmth out of his palm. His smile disappeared. We stared at one another, and his eyes began to open wide.

"What are you doing to him?" the other said, gripping my wrist. I turned and placed my hand gently on his, pulling the warmth out, as well.

All at once, I let go, and they snapped their hands back, rubbing them.

"This is the last place you want to be right now," I said.

They immediately walked into the street, taking turns looking back at me.

I made my way past the monks to the front door. Franklyn stared at me.

I unlocked the door and stepped inside. April was standing at the front bay window, looking at the lawn. The bruises were all gone. "What did you do to those kids?"

"Reasoned with them."

"All morning, they were—"

I gently swiveled her around by the shoulders. Our eyes locked. I pressed my lips to hers. She snaked her hands up my back, her body pressing into mine.

"They're both asleep, you said?" I whispered, caressing the hair away from her ear.

She nodded.

I carried her upstairs, setting her down in the guest bedroom. She closed the door, turned off the light, and drew the curtains. I lost track of her in the darkness until I heard a soft rustling as she took off her miniskirt and blouse. I folded my clothes, as well, placing them on the club chair by the bed.

It would be a brief respite, a short breather of the type that only lovers could provide one another, a time with no hurt feelings or disappointments; no discussion of our future or the lack thereof; no agendas. It would be a time to give the other pleasure in a world that was so unfair, so terribly hurtful and violent, a world overflowing with betrayal and lacking in any lasting fulfillment, a world that Grandfather soon would be leaving. It would be a small break from all that, a slow and gentle pause before going back to the harshness of everything. A time of simple lovemaking.

Afterward, she lay on her back. There was a small amount of light creeping through the curtains. The perspiration on her forehead and above her lip glistened.

I took her hand and interlaced the fingers in mine. "I feel like talking about the martial arts," I said.

She stared at the ceiling, laughing. "That's what comes to mind?"

"No, really. I've dedicated my life to this. I want to explain it to you. I want you to understand why all of it is worth dedicating a life to. I want you to understand this part of me, of Grandfather."

She caressed the underside of her breast with the back of her fingertips in a slow, semi-circular motion. "It's always been so much gibberish to me."

"You also need to know because this will be the life I intend to offer Fletcher, if he wants it."

"Okay."

"Suppose I have a little, blond, eight-year-old girl who earns a green belt in karate. By the green-belt level, her mom has seen me teach her to kick and punch; break one pine board with her tiny fist; do some forms, spar with other kids her size; and so on, the same as any other karate school. So, the mom is happy because her little girl is gaining confidence and maybe learning to defend herself against a pedophile and all the rest of it.

"And that's all true, but it's completely peripheral to the really important stuff we're teaching beneath the surface, so to speak. You see, what the mom doesn't know, and the little girl certainly doesn't realize yet at her age, is that we're sneaking into the training some very important universal truths about how to live life in a world filled to the brim with adversaries, small and large. We're teaching this little girl life lessons under the radar."

"Like what?" April said.

"When someone attacks, you step out of the way. You don't meet their force with your force. You leverage your attacker's power against himself. You don't deal with an attack in straight lines. You use torque—"

"What's torque?" she said.

"Leveraged twisting. You maintain inner balance. You never panic. You don't just react to an attack. You respond, meaning you think first. Big difference. And you don't destroy your opponent. You use the least force necessary to subdue him. You show compassion for your adversary.

"Later, after that little girl has left karate behind and gone on to replace it with ballet and soccer, these basic lessons of how to deal with an adversary remain embedded somewhere in her mind."

"As does the self-defense, right?"

"Truthfully, as she becomes a teenager and then an adult, she will rarely find herself needing to punch and kick people."

"Sometimes, she might."

"Yes, but very rarely. The far more likely adversarial scenario is that she will find herself in a situation with a boss who is angry at her for something she was not responsible for, or her teenage boy is stealing petty cash from her pocketbook, or she gets cancer. Her response to the pummeling of life hopefully will be flexible and balanced, to not struggle. She will hopefully approach it without anger, using leverage and intelligence. In other words, she will apply the martial arts principles she first learned as an eight-year-old green belt.

"She won't even remember that these were things we first taught her so long ago, and certainly our lessons will have been reinforced by other life experiences since. But we started it all. We served as the forgotten introduction.

We began the process of showing a small child the way to keep her head while floating in a sea of threats, to yield to the current of life without surrender."

"Beautiful," April said, grazing the underside of my chin, "and all that from what she learned in a karate school?"

"Learning how to handle an adversarial situation with grace and wisdom is a lesson of incredibly broad application. It's a seed. Someday, it sprouts, and who even remembers who planted it?"

"And you never get credit?"

"Usually not. But what's the difference? We're not in this to get credit."

"What about the adult students?"

"The advanced ones, by the time they get to brown-belt level and certainly at the black-belt level, we begin to teach them the internal techniques. We begin to teach them about the *chi*. We slowly show them the dynamic principles of life."

"The power to heal."

"In part. Through the martial arts, we begin to provide our advanced students with the opportunity to become aware, really aware. We give them the chance—though honestly, most of them don't take us up on it in any sustained way—to gain insight into great universal truths. We go beyond how to deal with adversarial situations. We offer a way to understand life itself."

"And how many—?"

The bedroom door swung open. Jaegyu stepped inside and flipped on the lights. He was wearing a gray suit and black tie and held a semiautomatic handgun. It was aimed at April.

"Who the fuck are you?" she shrieked, sitting up and pulling the cover over her breasts.

He followed her movement with the gun. "Be quiet, whore."

I sat up. "What do you want?"

He kept his gun aimed at April, looking directly at her but speaking to me. "Where is Jason Heung?"

"Look, Jaegyu, I'm done with all that. I no longer work for the Heungs. Go protect them or kill them or anything in-between. I don't care. I'm a civilian now."

He clenched his jaw, but otherwise, gave off no reaction. "I repeat, where is Jason Heung?"

"If I tell you, will you leave?"

"Where is—?"

Grandfather stepped behind Jaegyu and lightly touched his wrist. The gun dropped to the floor. Jaegyu rubbed his fingers, and turned, reaching toward Grandfather's neck.

Grandfather waved the air in front of him. Jaegyu immediately collapsed to the floor.

I rolled out of bed and grabbed the gun, dislodging the clip. April came up behind me, draping a too-small robe over my shoulders. "I thought you were asleep," I said to Grandfather, tying the sash around my waist.

"Awake now," he said, kneeling next to Jaegyu, whose eyes were catatonic. "What is this about?"

I knelt, as well. "Susan Heung had some sort of alliance with this man, or he was infiltrating her organization to destroy it from within—I never figured out which. He's wanted to kill me for a long time. But regardless, Susan's brother, who we thought was dead, is actually turning state's evidence against the South Korean interests this man represents. He wants Jason Heung killed. He was demanding that I tell him where he is."

Grandfather's long, tangled gray and black hair rested on his shoulders. His brown eyes were soft and gentle. They reminded me of when I was that eight-year-old with the green belt learning from this giant of a man. "This will be the last lesson I teach you," Grandfather said.

He positioned his fingers on Jaegyu's wrist and massaged. Eventually, Jaegyu blinked and looked at Grandfather and then me. "What did you do to me?" Jaegyu said.

"You threatened to kill my wife and my two sons," Grandfather said.

April glanced at me. She had heard it too.

Two sons.

"I cannot allow that," Grandfather said.

"Are you going to kill me?" Jaegyu said.

"I am going to give you an imbalance in the toe of your right foot. It will be a dull pain that cannot be alleviated with medication or massage or any other external means. Most days, it will cause nothing more than a slight limp. Over time, it will grow worse. In six months, it will become unbearable. There will be only one way to reduce the pain and bring it back to just a distant ache. That will be to seek out my son and have him give you treatment. But of course, six months after that, you will need another, and so on. The pain will be so intense at those intervals that you will do anything for him to alleviate it. You will give him any amount of money, perform any service. But all he will ask of you is that you not harm him, his wife, or his son. If you harm any of them, you will continue to suffer with the pain until you finally take your own life to stop the agony."

Grandfather took my hand and placed it on the large toe of Jaegyu's right foot. "Pull out the warmth for a count of five," he whispered. "Then place your other hand on the back of the toe and force the warmth back in. One hand pulling and the other pushing. Like this." Grandfather clapped his hands together and held them up, open palmed. "Just like that."

"How does this work?" I said.

"The second hand will disrupt the flow of energy from the first, creating an imbalance."

"And how do I stop his pain in later months?"

"Just do the first part without the second. Suck out the warmth. It will rebalance the joint temporarily."

I looked at Jaegyu. "You did this to yourself."

"Fuck you."

I placed my hand on his foot and breathed deeply.

Grandfather started counting, "One, two, three, four five...close."

I clapped my other hand to the foot and forced heat back in. Jaegyu's back arched, and he grimaced.

I pulled my hands away, holding them up, open palmed as Grandfather had done.

Grandfather hooked his hand under Jaegyu's armpit and helped him up. "Listen to me," Grandfather said. "Each time my son does this, he will determine whether you are ready to give up this threat against my family. If so, he will also have the knowledge necessary to cure you completely. Your only obligation from that point forward will be to never again seek to cause them harm. Do you understand?"

Jaegyu clenched his jaw but said nothing.

Grandfather let go of him. "You may leave."

I followed Jaegyu onto the second floor landing, watching him negotiate the stairs one at a time. He did not look back, but went straight out the front door. I stepped to the window and watched him walk past the monks, limping slightly. The monks stopped chanting and watched him, as well. Once he was gone, they looked up at the window, staring at me.

Grandfather took my hand. "To completely heal him, simply do the first part three times in succession."

"And what do you plan on doing for the rest of today?"

"Sleep."

CHAPTER TWENTY-SIX

The next morning, April and Fletcher stood on the front lawn by the door. She was wearing a shoulder-to-toe white gown, the color of mourning in the Chinese tradition. Fletcher was dressed in a white, button-down shirt and pants.

There were about two dozen monks facing them, kneeling on the grass in a loose semicircle. The monks were singing a chant I had never heard before. It was soft and melodic, in a sad minor key. They shook their incense sticks between their open palms in a coordinated rhythm.

Bette and I stood in the back, behind the monks. She held a small bit of tissue in her fist.

After a while, I saw Pauline park across the street. I moved to the side to make room for her. She stepped over a patch of yellow and white marigolds, joining us.

"So, this is it?" she said over the chanting.

"In a manner of speaking," I said. "He's going to give his Last Statement and then we'll go inside for the Last Celebration."

She took off her designer sunglasses and folded them into a pink clutch. "Then what? Pills, a knife to slit the wrists, what?"

"Nothing so dramatic. He'll just go upstairs and sleep to death."

"While the rest of us remain downstairs and sip punch?"

"Essentially."

"You'll have to explain all this to me someday."

"Someday, not now."

"And you, my karate girl," Pauline said, putting her arm around Bette, "please don't cry."

"Can't help it," Bette said, looking away.

Pauline held her more tightly. "Things will all work out."

"How do you know?"

"They always do."

Fletcher was getting restless. I saw April lift him and whisper in his ear. She brought him with her as she joined us.

"Real private moment with all the monks here," she said to me.

"Come on, April. We're getting to the finish line."

She stroked the back of Fletcher's head. He struggled, and she put him down. He ran to the front and picked up a red plastic airplane.

"You want me to get him?" I said.

"No, leave him be." April said. She turned to Pauline. "Thanks for being here. I know it means a lot to him."

"I'm glad I could attend," Pauline said. "Not sure what this is all about, but I know how important it is. You ever hear from that guy Len again?"

"No, and good riddance," April said.

"Amen."

"You know," April said, "I was thinking last night of when I first met Grandfather at the dungeon, after you hired him as a bouncer. What was that, six years ago?"

"Something like that," Pauline said.

"He looked so goofy with his long hair going every which way and his Hawaiian shirt never tucked in. One evening after a really busy shift, I was completely drained. He came by and placed his hand on my tummy. That's when I felt the warmth for the first time."

"The *chi*," I said.

"Yeah," April paused. "It's so fucked up that he's doing this." She turned to me. "I really want to hate him, Lock."

"I know," I replied.

"It's so goddamn selfish," she said.

"He would not disagree."

"And Fletcher will lose a father. Why does it have to be this way?"

"You keep asking me that, and I don't really have an answer."

She craned her head to see Fletcher. The little boy appeared oblivious. "How much longer?" she said.

"Franklyn might know."

"The crazy monk? Can you go talk to him, please?"

Across the street, some older ladies stopped to stare. They were eating ice cream. One had a Labrador Retriever by the leash.

I walked to the center of the lawn. Franklyn was surrounded by his fellow monks. There were a number of knotted, wooden prayer beads circled around his neck. "When will he begin his witness?" I said.

"Soon. Are you ready to take over the System?"

Take over the System—how could I even presume to do that? In every sense of the word, I was a student of it still. But now, as I had told Bette she might have to do if I were not around, ready or not, I would need to step up. It would be far more than instructing the little blond green belts. I would be responsible for all the schools that quietly practiced Grandfather's System; from New Jersey to Colorado to Hawaii and a host of places in-between.

"Yes, I am."

I rejoined Bette, Pauline, and April. The chanting grew in intensity. "So?" April said.

"Soon," I replied.

Eventually, Grandfather stepped outside the house and held up his hand. The chanting stopped. "There are two rooms," he said. "We are all in the first, but one by one, each of us walks to the other, at our own pace and in our own time.

"As we do, more of us will be born and enter that first room. In the blink of an eye, all who are now in the first room will have moved to the second. Yet the first will still be populated by people behind us, many of whom are now yet unborn. All of life and death is simply moving from one room to the next. In this way, we are connected as boarders in the same dwelling. We inhabit a grand mansion of rooms unending. Therefore, this is not good-bye. I assure you we will meet again somewhere in our common dwelling, that place of infinite rooms. That mansion that houses all of Humanity.

"This mansion has been created by the many billions who have lived and are living. It reflects the sum total of our consciousness, of our civilization, our history. We serve as both its architects and inhabitants.

"In the course of our lives, each of us is free to paint our room with any combination of colors, pleasing or clashing or none at all. We can leave it as we found it or change it completely. We can rip apart the small corner of the room in which we dwell, or we can preserve and treat it with reverence. It is a joint undertaking, and no one of us controls the ultimate result of what this room will become.

"If you find yourself confused and overwhelmed by the immensity of this artistic undertaking, I can tell you that the first step is to fill your heart with compassion. That is and always will be the starting point. From there, you may take the work of building this common dwelling in any direction you wish, for the world inhabits you as much as you inhabit it.

"Let your heart guide you, and a masterpiece will soon emerge. That is my statement."

He motioned to Fletcher, who was still playing with the toy airplane. "My child is now in your hands. I ask you to care for and nurture him as he grows into manhood. Protect him, train him, and eventually, if he proves worthy, follow him."

Grandfather held out his hand in April's direction. She came to the front and joined him. "This is his mother. I exhort you to care for her, as well."

He motioned to me. "And this is the new head of our System. He will oversee and develop it. In all things relating to the System, trust him. He will guide you."

Grandfather waved his hand in a long arc. "Now, come inside. Let us feast and celebrate as you send me off on my voyage."

He led us into the house. The dining room was packed with all manner of Chinese delicacies. There were fruits and vegetables, rice cakes, sweetened almonds, and honey cookies. Papier-mâché dragons and butterflies hung from the ceiling. There were posters of five immense Japanese letters tacked to the wall, the sacred symbols of Reiki. The one in the center was *Dai Ko Myo*.

Master.

I served the monks green tea. They each bowed in turn. Grandfather passed out plates. Fletcher held onto Grandfather's thigh. Eventually, Grandfather took the small boy in his arms.

April stood on tiptoe and wrapped her arms around both of them, closing her eyes and swaying back and forth.

As I approached, Grandfather put Fletcher down, and we embraced.

"I don't know what I'll do without you," I said, holding him tightly.

"Take the System where you feel it should go. Put your imprint on it. Then give it to Fletcher when he is ready, if he's worthy, and if he wants it."

"And then I'll be free to start sleeping twenty hours a day."

"Something much more than sleep, Little One. The day the Buddha achieved enlightenment, he went to a local village. A man saw him and sensed something. He asked the Buddha if he was a wizard, a magician, or perhaps a king, and the Buddha laughed and said no to all of those things. But there is definitely something different about you, the villager said. What is it? And the Buddha replied, 'I am awake.'"

"We sleep to death to awaken," I said.

"Exactly. Take care of her and the new Little One."

"I will. I promise."

"Which does not mean you should shield them from all of life's hurts," he said. "Just do what you can, and in all things, be gentle with yourself."

He turned to April. "Ready, love of my life?"

"Yes," she replied. Her tone was different. Dignified and poised.

"Come with us, Fletcher," Grandfather said, lifting him again.

Fletcher hugged Grandfather's neck. "I don't want you to go."

"We'll see each other again soon enough. I promise."

Grandfather turned and said to the others, "I now leave for the second part of this celebration, which is taking place in the next world. A celebration of this life awaits me there, filled with old friends and relatives, with adversaries and distant acquaintances, the sum total of those who participated in my life and have left this world before me. Rest assured that I shall also welcome each of you to your own such celebrations in due course. We shall certainly meet again."

The monks began to chant louder. Grandfather took April's hand. I watched the three of them go upstairs to Grandfather's room.

&

People began to leave. Eventually, they were all gone. The living room was silent.

April walked down the stairs. She placed her hand gently on my forehead. "How are you?" she said.

"Drained. And him?"

"I just called the ambulance to take his body to the funeral home. Yesterday, he gave me a sealed envelope with written instructions. He wants his ashes released in Hawaii, the Buddhist temple at Kauai Island where Fletcher was born. He wants you there too. He signed a certificate of some type. It promotes you to tenth-degree black belt in Shaolin Kempo Karate and confirms that the internal System has been bequeathed to you as the Head Master Instructor."

"How's Fletcher?"

"Come and see for yourself. Grandfather did something to calm him somehow."

She took my hand, interlacing her fingers in mine. As we walked up the stairs, she stroked it with her thumb. Fletcher was sitting on the hallway carpet putting together a jigsaw puzzle.

"So, now the monks leave?" April said, looking out the window.

"They are probably off to prepare a service for him," I replied, standing behind him and inspecting the puzzle.

"Help me finish," Fletcher said.

I knelt next to him. "Of course."

CHAPTER TWENTY-SEVEN

April accepted a bungalow from the monks at the Hongwanji Mission on Kauai Island. It was where Grandfather had developed the System and where the in-gathering for his death ceremony would take place the following week.

The Shinto Buddhist Temple was in the center of the mission, located on a cliff overlooking the Pacific Ocean. The monks had cleared a spot where mourners could spread the ashes of their loved ones below.

I followed April as she and Fletcher walked to the edge of the outcropping. April knelt and unscrewed the pewter receptacle, handing it to Fletcher. He turned it over, allowing the ashes to sprinkle down to the white-capped blue waves.

Franklyn was now wearing abbot's robes. I had not realized he was the head of the mission. The fact that he had spent so much time chanting on a small lawn in Edgewater, New Jersey, spoke volumes about Grandfather's importance to Franklyn's order.

Afterward, April and Fletcher joined Franklyn on a stone bench. April motioned me to join them.

"Explain it again so Lock can hear too," she said.

"Nirvana is not a place," Franklyn replied. "It is the absence of place. It is a state of enlightenment that supersedes the illusion of place."

"Say more about it," she said.

"This world is a place. To get beyond it is to advance beyond the illusion. What is inside of us, what animates us, is real. But that is not the part we see. It is inaccessible to most. To a few, it is a fleeting glimpse of something larger. To Grandfather, a Bodhisattva, it was home. Your child has the same potential."

April was quiet, running her hand through Fletcher's hair. "So, how do I help him develop it?"

"Love him."

"What else?"

"Train him."

"He's four years old."

"He is."

She took a deep breath. "I keep having to say that to everyone."

"It is true."

"Where would we train him? Here?"

"Where is not important, though there will always be a place for him here, if he wants it, and a place for you too, good woman."

"You would take me in after the way I treated you?"

"Without hesitation," he said, laughing.

❧

The next morning, I woke next to April. It was cool and dark. The sun was rising over the ocean. I opened a window and let the breeze enter our room. April pulled the covers to her neck and watched me. I came back and crawled under them, embracing her.

"I was thinking," I said, "if we were to get married, we might do it here, at the temple. Franklyn could officiate."

She smiled. "I was having the same thought."

We had breakfast on the deck behind the bungalow. April prepared vegetable egg white omelets for the three of us. I poured Fletcher mango juice and made mimosas for April and me.

"So," she said, "if we're becoming sort of engaged now, maybe we should talk about household finances."

"Sure."

"You're the Head Master Instructor of the System," she said, taking a forkful of her omelet. "Does that pay?"

"I don't think of it in those terms," I said.

"But if you did," she said, biting into her toast, "like for example, what does a master do?"

"Funny question for you to be asking."

"You know what I mean."

"There are eighteen schools that are run by Grandfather's students, many of whom you'll be meeting next week at the memorial service we're having here. My small school, or really Bette's, is one of them. There is a very loose affiliation. Some of us have joint tournaments and award ceremonies and such. That stuff doesn't interest me much. It's kind of standard karate fare that you would see in most martial arts schools. But there's a small cluster of elite black belts who Grandfather secretly trained over the years in the internal arts—advanced private seminars and such. A few are here, in Hawaii. Some others are in Colorado, for whatever reason. I would go with him sometimes to assist. He stopped doing it in the last couple of years. Maybe I'll start it up again. Also, as part of my duties, I'll make decisions on high-ranking belt promotions and address the rancor that sometimes surrounds it."

She drank some juice. "But the belts only apply to the Shaolin Kempo Karate system, not the other, the Qi Gong and Reiki, right?"

"Impressive, April."

"And I'm not calling it Judo anymore."

"Even more impressive."

She leaned in and whispered. "I always knew it wasn't Judo. I just liked to see you get your panties in a twist." She poured me more juice. "So, again, do you get paid for any of this?"

"Nothing to speak of. My travel expenses, and they pool a small honorarium for the workshops. Grandfather never wanted to turn it all into a franchise. He felt it would demean the principles of the System, especially the internal part."

"Grandfather was never good with money," she replied, "I was the sole breadwinner. The New Jersey house is in my name. I would even give him a small weekly allowance, for Christ's sake."

"Well," I said, "since that's already in the household budget—"

"Yeah, I figured that part out already."

"And just how much do you pull in at the dungeon?" I said.

"Maybe thirty thousand and another thirty or so freelance."

"Without Pauline knowing about the freelance."

"Let's not go there again, please."

"And you bought the house with that?"

"It's an all-cash business, so that helps. Also, even though it's in Edgewater, it's a very small house, and there's a big mortgage on it. I only had to put five percent down, because the seller took back the mortgage. We didn't go through a bank. What about you?"

"The karate school nets about twenty five per year. My bodyguarding was another forty or so, but that's mostly gone now for obvious reasons."

"And you're giving up the school to Bette. You're not selling it to her; you're giving it to her, correct?"

"Right, I need to focus on re-building the System."

"And the Susan Heung bodyguarding part of your income is pretty much done with at this point."

"As I said, I would think so."

"So, you have no financial prospects to speak of?"

"Essentially, other than a small police pension."

"So, the bottom line is that there is no bottom line."

"Want to bail yet?" I said.

She sipped her mango juice. "And change my self-destructive approach to relationships with men? Never."

Fletcher ran into the room and jumped on my lap. "I want to learn karate."

"You do?" I said.

"Teach me."

My cell phone vibrated. The caller I.D. read Anonymous. "Hello?" I said.

"I just got here, and figured I'd look up old friends." It was Len's voice.

"What do you mean you got here?" I said.

"I'm in a hotel about twenty minutes from you."

"What the hell are you doing in Hawaii?"

"Come to my hotel, and I'll tell you. I'd go to you, but I assume your little bitch might not want to see me."

"Safe assumption, and don't call her that."

"Fine, sure, just come over. We have to talk."

જી

Len met me in the lobby of his hotel. He was wearing a floral print shirt, totally different from his usual black slacks and gray dress shirt. We stopped in the gift shop so he could buy a straw hat to keep the sun out of his eyes. It had the words *Born to Surf* emblazoned across the front.

The waves created an uneven border of white suds on the sand. Occasionally, we had to zigzag to avoid getting our feet wet.

"You know, Len," I said. "I have a feeling you're here to tell me something that will not make me happy."

"Depends," he said. "Hey, before we get into all that, are there any good whorehouses down here? I never fucked a Hawaiian girl before."

"I notice that you tend to objectify women."

"Just trying to taste all the food groups, Lock. Never had a Hawaiian before. Can't find one in a Newark whorehouse, obviously."

"And whose fault is that?"

He smiled. "It's all mental with me. Ever since I was little, I always wanted what I didn't have. That's the reason the more a bitch hates me, the more I want her. I just love to anger fuck. I find it invigorating."

"Ever try anger management?"

He laughed. "As a matter of fact, when I was a Fair Lawn detective, there was an incident, and the union cut a deal for me to attend anger management therapy sessions given by a cute little Puerto Rican social worker. It worked. After I fucked her, I wasn't as angry."

"For those who are open to it, therapy can be a life-affirming endeavor."

"Actually, I like to think of myself as a kind of therapist too. I take bitches under my wing and mentor them. Remember when I surmised that your ex-wife didn't know about the frenulum, how she should be using her tongue ...?"

"Oh, Jesus fuck, Len..."

"Well, I never resolved that one with her, thanks to you. But there are plenty of other ones who need to learn ..."

"You came down here to waste my time with this bullshit?"

"Just listen. I looked into this. People are born with different ways of learning. With most bitches, it's tactile. They learn by holding things in their hands, big black hard things."

I stared at him.

He shrugged.

"You done?" I said.

"There's actually another reason it's worth investing the time and effort to teach bitches how to give proper blowjobs."

"Wait a minute. You like blowjobs? How come you never mentioned it before?"

"It's so we don't have to abstain when she's during her woman time."

"Would you excuse me for a moment while I step into the ocean to vomit?"

"Listen, Lock, I do need to talk to you about something."

"So now, the serious Len."

"Yeah, we're pivoting."

"No more exploration of relationship issues?"

"Yeah, yeah, listen to me. Cousin Bodacious wants to offer you a job, freelance security under me."

"Wouldn't that be a bit awkward, given my bodyguarding work for Susan Heung?"

"You mean Prisoner Number 76923A? What are you going to do, sit in a cell with her at the Edna Mahan Correctional Facility and guard her from voracious lesbians?"

"Cho can't get her out on bail?"

Len picked up a small stick and threw it into the surf. "They won't give her bail because they're afraid she'll use her dual South Korean citizenship and flee the country. She's got a residence there, also offices and such. She is what you might call a flight risk."

"So they're serious about prosecuting her?"

"Her brother, Jason, gave them a perfect road map."

"The man you swore to me was dead."

"That was my information at the time."

"And somehow by coincidence this entire situation ended up in Cousin Bodacious's favor. The Heungs being taken down; Jason Heung making his way out of that prison without being shot so he could testify against his sister; Cho's next congressional run being stopped in its tracks. That's a lot of coincidences."

"You're not in jail. Maybe that's also not a coincidence. Maybe we protected you."

"Out of the kindness of your heart?"

"No, because we saw your talent and wanted to leave open the possibility of your working for us. You know, Cousin Bodacious has been endlessly replaying the surveillance tape of your little tiff with the Rapid Response Team at East Jersey Prison. He even forced me to sit through it a few times. You defeated a pack of heavily armed and armored law-enforcement officers. Your hands were so fast at times that even frame by frame, we couldn't follow what you did. It was like a tornado dropped down and flung them all in a million directions, and you didn't even take a shot."

"Maybe you can package it in a DVD, *Ex-husbands Fight Corrupt Law Enforcement Officers*, volume 2257."

"Cousin Bodacious was very impressed. He personally directed me to come here and extend you the offer for freelance work. He wants you to say yes."

"To play a part in what I assume will be Cousin Bodacious's effort to take over what used to be the Heung drug trade in Bergen County."

"Hey, great idea."

"Sam Attia will come after you full force, like he did the Russians years ago and then the Koreans."

"We're not them."

"What about the South Korean mob that the Heungs were using for their supply line? Will they just step aside politely?"

"It's not the South Korean mob," he said. "There is no South Korean mob in New Jersey. It's a rogue element in the South Korean State Intelligence. They call it NIS. Big difference."

"Fine, NIS, whatever."

"The Heungs were dealing with former NIS people through the Bank of Korea, even though there isn't really such a thing as 'former' in that line of work. The bank itself is clean, but these jokers have infiltrated a small part of it without the people who run it knowing. Rumor is that NIS secretly uses it as a front for money laundering and can guarantee no interruption in the supply, no interdiction by the Korean government. They're jacked in."

"And now they are just going to step aside and let Bodacious take over?"

"Quite the opposite. We're cutting them in on a very generous split. They hate people with our complexion, but green trumps black every time. If all goes well, within a year, we could be making them a nice chunk of change each month. It helped convince them to forgo their vengeance against us for how everything worked out so badly for the Heungs."

"So all the criminals are playing nicely again. And why would I want to get back into that cesspool after I just got out?"

"A few reasons. First, I'm willing to pay you two thousand dollars as a flat fee every time I use you for a job. That can be for one hour of your time just milling in the crowd undercover while Cousin Bodacious attends the groundbreaking for one of his many drug treatment centers, or it could be a week while he visits with one of the many bitches fortunate enough to be invited to his compound in the Catoctin Mountains in Maryland."

"Virginia."

"His compound is on the Maryland side."

"I didn't know the Catoctins extended into Maryland."

"So, now you know. If you get fifty of those jobs a year, you're making in the six figures. And it can go up from there. Second, I'm going to personally intercede on your behalf and convince Kim Jaegyu not to kill you, your bitch and her kid."

"I told you not to call her my bitch."

"He's targeting the three of you as we speak."

"Jaegyu is...?"

"Yeah, he's here."

"In Hawaii, now?"

"Yeah, he's about to kill you, rape your female—I assume that term is acceptable?"

"Barely."

"And make her kid watch before he throws him over the cliff where his father's ashes were just spread. It would have happened already, but I convinced him to hold off to see if I could intercede. That's another reason I'm in Hawaii."

"Why does Jaegyu want to kill me to avenge Susan Heung? That makes no sense if the NIS has cut a deal with Cousin Bodacious. He's switched sides. What does he care?"

"Apparently you fucked up his foot. Is that right?"

"Grandfather fucked up his foot. I can't take the credit."

"Well, regardless, he's been walking in pain ever since. He's gone to a bunch of specialists, and no one can diagnose the problem, much less fix it. They're talking about amputating his toe. You humiliated him."

"So, I'll fix his toe, and we call it even?"

"No, you fix his toe, pay him fifty thousand dollars and that will almost make it even. I'll get him to accept."

"I don't have fifty thousand dollars."

"Consider it a sign-on bonus and to make the runaround we inadvertently gave you on the Jason Heung thing square between us."

"Along those lines, just what was Cousin Bodacious's connection to the attempt on Jason Heung?"

"This again? Really?"

"Come on, just once and for all, tell me the whole story."

"We looked for him, and we should have been able to find him, since we controlled the prison. But Bergenweld completely fucked us on that score. He's the one who assured us Jason had been killed. I didn't lie to you. I was lied to."

"Bergenweld lied to you because he was aligned with Attia."

"When it started to become clear that Jason Heung might still be alive, the NIS stopped talking to us and did their own investigation. They confirmed Jason was alive, but they had no idea where he was. Since we got it wrong, they were convinced we were full of shit—either we were playing both sides or just incompetent."

"Finally somebody else is accused of incompetence."

He stopped walking and gripped my elbow. "Hey, you're not incompetent. You're the best bodyguard I've ever seen, and a hell of a good private detective. Believe me, we would not be making this offer if we thought you were incompetent."

"Thanks, Len. That's definitely a boost to my self-esteem."

"I mean it. You're good at what you do. Don't ever think otherwise."

"You'd make a good life coach."

"Noticed that too?" His laugh slipped into a wheezing cough. "Anyway, the bottom line is that NIS concluded we were incapable of helping them. So, they instructed Jaegyu to stop negotiating with us until the matter was resolved. He went around us and enlisted Susan Heung to assist however she could, figuring that the NIS's interests were aligned with hers. But in the end, he lost faith in her too and ended up working around the Heungs, as well. He didn't trust anyone at that point. He decided to do the whole thing on his own. That's when he interviewed the cellmate."

"And killed him?"

"I don't know, and I don't care," he said.

"Either way, he's a mentally fucked up little prick."

"You don't know the half of it. Look up his name on the Internet."

"Why?" I said.

"He named himself after one of the most notorious assassins in South Korean history. It was like an American calling himself Lee Harvey Oswald. But since we're not Korean, none of us knew that. It was like he was laughing in our faces, mocking our stupidity by making it clear that he was a deranged scumbag assassin without our realizing it. Hiding in plain sight."

"Does Attia know any of this?"

"Doesn't really matter. Law enforcement can't have Jaegyu arrested. He has diplomatic immunity, can be accused by American law enforcement of a crime, but not convicted. He would have to be tried in South Korea."

"Which would never happen," I said.

"Or if it did happen, he wouldn't be found guilty. But that's all water under the bridge. He's partnering with us now, and I want you two to play nicely together, as you said.

Anyway, you going to take Cousin Bodacious's generous offer or what?"

"Let me speak to my female about it first."

"Fine, but you need to give me an answer in twenty-four hours. After that, you're on your own with Jaegyu."

CHAPTER TWENTY-EIGHT

It was early evening. I was sitting on the couch with April, staring at the fireplace. Fletcher was in his room watching television.

April entwined her fingers with mine. I ran my other hand along her thigh.

"What did the creep talk to you about?" she said.

"He wanted me to direct him to the best Hawaiian girls in the area. He's got money to spend."

"I've heard that some girls actually like money being spent on them."

"But not you," I said.

"Well, that's true of course. I have very little interest in fine jewelry and designer clothes."

"Good thing too."

"You know he's a complete creep."

I got up and tossed another log on the fire. The ocean breeze was strong. I brought over a cover for us. "The creep offered me a job," I said. "Six-figure potential."

"Doing what?" she said.

"Freelance bodyguarding for Cousin Bodacious."

"And you turned him down, of course."

"I said I would talk it over with you."

"Oh, come on."

"We need the money," I said.

"I told you. I'm fine being the breadwinner."

"I'm not. Don't you want the option of retiring from doing sessions at the dungeon, just being my future wife, Fletcher's mother, just chilling for a while? Don't you at least deserve that option?"

She stared at the fireplace. One of the logs split in half, sending sparks upward. "I don't want you working for the man who beat me."

"I'm not thrilled about that part either. But you remember that guy who broke into the house and was going to shoot us?"

"Of course."

"Len can pay him off to leave us alone."

"You can't just do that toe-thing on the rest of him?"

"Maybe, but he has others working with him who would also come after us. I can't fight an army of Korean intelligence agents worldwide. And even if I could, I can't also protect you and Fletcher at the same time. They'll get to us eventually if they're determined. There's just too many of them."

"So, we make two pacts with the devil, the guy who beat me up and the guy who almost took a shot at the two of us?"

"Yeah, peace in our time. It worked so well in World War II."

"And you are okay going back to working with criminals, after all that back and forth about how you weren't like them and wanted to get out and all the rest of it?"

"I'm not saying I want to do it. I'm saying I may have to do it for us. Family is about sacrifice. I'm sacrificing to protect Fletcher and you."

"And what about our plans to live out here permanently?"

"They will have to change temporarily. We'll need to go back to Jersey. I'll need to be on call for Cousin Bodacious." I closed my eyes. "Just saying that makes me cringe."

"How about a counteroffer? We never go back to Jersey? We stay here forever and just disappear?"

"Sure, I'll shave my head and become a monk."

She sat up. "And be abstinent?"

"Would that be a problem?"

She shrugged. "Not really, no."

"What do you think Grandfather would say about all this?" I said.

"He'd just laugh and change the subject."

"He did have a terrific laugh."

We were silent for a long while. The fire decreased to a red glow on the underside of the logs. A slight odor of smoke permeated the room. "You're going to do it, aren't you?" she said.

"I have no choice really."

"It's all so sad. Can't you think of any way to make all the bad things go away, just for a moment?"

"Sure I can, but what if the kid comes in?"

"If he comes in, just say you're teaching me Judo."

I tickled her. "Learn anything yet?"

She shrieked, tickling me back. "Yeah, that you suck at Judo."

✦

The next morning, I sat on the edge of the bed, watching April snore softly. I picked up the phone and called Len at his hotel. "Did I wake you?" I said.

"I was in the middle of fucking my new Hawaiian girlfriend I met last night."

"So we're both in the process of getting fucked by you."

"Now that's funny."

"Make the deal with Jaegyu."

"Good choice. I'll need to bring him over so you can fix his toe. After all this, you can fix his fucking toe, can't you?"

"Pretty sure I can."

"In a couple of hours."

After he hung up, I stared at the phone. Fletcher opened the bedroom door and climbed onto the bed, straddling my lap. "You said you would teach me karate."

"You want to learn karate?" I said.

"Yeah."

"I'm not awake," April said.

"Now," Fletcher said.

April pulled the covers over her head. "Go outside, both of you."

❧

Fletcher and I ate a bowl of fruit and whole-wheat toast. We put the dishes in the sink and moved the chairs and table to the side of the deck.

The sun was coming up just over the temple cornices in the distance. Fletcher and I stood in the center of the deck, barefoot. I showed him the Shaolin salute, a fist behind an open palm. It was how Kempo Karate practitioners worldwide started their lessons. Peace over violence. "I'm going to teach you an easy and gentle way of getting rid of a bad man. We lift up the tree first and then we push it away, okay?"

"Yeah," he said.

"Once we lift it, we can throw it as far as we want." I knelt and put both hands on his stomach, pushing upward gently. He took a few steps back. "You feel that?"

"Yeah."

"You push up first, then out. Try it."

Even kneeling, I was a few inches taller than him. He placed his hands on my abdomen and pushed upward and out. I leaned back with the movement. "That's it."

For the next half hour, I pushed him and he pushed back again and again. I corrected some of his movements, but he caught on quickly.

It was a feat for most kids that age just to differentiate between pushing forward and pushing up and forward. That was the importance of the lesson. The strength to really do the technique would come years later. A select few might even learn to do it the way it was meant to be done, with *Jing*.

My knees were getting sore. "Just a few more," I said.

"Where is Grandfather?" he said, pushing my chest up and out.

"He's here. We just can't see him."

"Why?"

"Because he's no longer alive."

"How do you know he's here?"

"Don't you feel him?"

"No."

"You will."

"He told me that I would see him soon," he said.

"You will, but only after many years."

A lifetime.

"Are you my father now?"

"Do you want me to be?"

"Yeah."

"Then I am."

"I saw him last night in a dream," he said.

"What did he say?"

"He told me not to cry."

The front door bell rang. I brought Fletcher to our bedroom and left him in bed with April. If this went wrong,

I needed to be able to deal with it without worrying about protecting her or my little one.

My Little One.

I opened the door and went outside, closing it behind me. Len was there. We shook hands. Jaegyu was standing about thirty feet away, leaning against Len's rental car, holding a cane and glaring at me.

"He doesn't want to come into your home," Len said.

"Good, because I don't want him in my home."

"He wants you just to fix his foot and give him his money. Then he'll leave."

"Fine by me."

"How long will it take to fix his toe?"

"Three treatments in succession. I can do it now. Have him sit on the hood of your car. I just need access to his toe." I glanced at Jaegyu. He still was staring at me.

Len turned away so Jaegyu could not see him hand me a thick pile of money wrapped in white plastic. "This is fifty thousand dollars. Give it to him before you start the treatment so it's from you."

"Fine."

"Problem solved."

"Management is a bitch, huh, Len?"

"Brother, you don't know the half of it."

EPILOGUE

Just before we left Hawaii, April and I married. Franklyn conducted the service. Fletcher was best man.

It was now many months later. We were back in New Jersey, living in April's home. Bette was running the karate school. I had made travel arrangements for us to make a trip to Colorado. I was scheduled to give a seminar there to a gathering of all the schools in our System. April would be coming along too. I had asked her to start the proceedings with a call for a moment of silence in memory of Grandfather. What she did not know was that I had arranged to have the heads of the eighteen schools use it as an opportunity to present her with an honorary black belt. Bette would lead that part of the ceremony.

It was morning. April had woken up as usual by straddling me and holding my hands down. It was not exactly making love—more like wrestling with benefits.

The phone rang. I tried to unravel myself. "Got to answer that," I said.

"What?"

"The phone."

"Just let it go to voicemail," she said. "I'm trying to Judo you, for Christ's sake."

I craned my neck, checking the caller ID. "It's Len. I need to answer."

"I so hate that prick," she said, letting go of my wrists. She knelt forward and hit the pillow with her fist.

I picked up the phone. "In the middle of something, Len."

"Not Len, it's Cousin Bodacious. I'm using Len's phone. This is Tourmaline, right?"

"Yes," I said, "what's going on?"

"How quickly can you get yourself to my place in Newark?"

I dislodged my leg from under April and sat up. "Immediately, if you need me. What's going on?"

"No good shit, I assure you," he said. "Just get some clothes on and get down here right now."

"I need to know what the situation is."

"Len was just shot by some chick."

Oh, Jesus. "Did anyone see who it was?"

"A white chick, that's all we know. I need you to take over temporarily as head of my security detail. Assignment number one is to find the bitch and bring her white ass to me. Got it?"

"I'll be down immediately."

"To me, Tourmaline. You find her and bring her ass to me." The line went dead.

I stood, lifting my watch from the nightstand and slipping it on. "Got to go to Newark," I said.

"And I've got to pee," she said, walking into the bathroom and leaving the door slightly ajar. "What's the emergency about?"

"Lori."

"Again?"

"Yeah, it never ends."

— Finis —

Made in the USA
Charleston, SC
04 November 2015